Alfred Austin

Rome or Death!

Alfred Austin

Rome or Death!

ISBN/EAN: 9783744787994

Printed in Europe, USA, Canada, Australia, Japan

Cover: Foto ©Andreas Hilbeck / pixelio.de

More available books at **www.hansebooks.com**

ROME OR DEATH!

ROME OR DEATH!

BY

ALFRED AUSTIN

WILLIAM BLACKWOOD AND SONS
EDINBURGH AND LONDON
MDCCCLXXIII

PRINTED BY WILLIAM BLACKWOOD AND SONS, EDINBURGH.

TO HIS EXCELLENCY

LORD ODO RUSSELL,

I DEDICATE

'ROME OR DEATH!'

IN IMPERFECT BUT CORDIAL TESTIMONY OF

HIS LOVE FOR ITALY,

HIS EMINENT PUBLIC SERVICES,

AND

HIS LONG-PROVED FRIENDSHIP FOR

THE AUTHOR.

PREFACE.

THE readers of 'Madonna's Child' will perhaps remember that it was professedly but an excerpt from the second of the four cantos, of which a poem, to be entitled 'The Human Tragedy,' will eventually consist. 'Rome or Death!' will form the third canto of the same work; but only in that sense is the one a continuation of the other. I should, however, add, that 'Madonna's Child' must be read before 'Rome or Death!' can be duly apprehended. When I next solicit the attention of my readers, it will be to submit to them 'The Human Tragedy' in its complete form.

It will soon be perceived that the following poem, even standing alone, is of a somewhat ambitious character; and I half cherish the hope that it may contribute at least towards solving affirmatively the question, so often propounded of late, whether the political events and emotions of our own time admit of poetical treatment by a contemporary writer. I venture to think that they do; whilst strongly inclining to the opinion that it is only very recently any such opportunity has been offered him. From 1815 to 1848 Europe deliberately elected to rest and be thankful; and though it then for a moment turned uneasily in its sleep, deep slumber once again shortly supervened, not to be fully shaken off till, in 1859, the sun of Italy rose over the horizon. From that hour to this, we have lived surely in as great and stirring an epoch as any ever relieved by the play of vigorous human passions; the last seven years, more especially, of the life of Europe, having been one continuous drama of the highest order, upon which the curtain has not yet fallen. Themes truly heroic once more swarm upon the imagination; and the difficulty is, not to find a subject, but to select from a host of subjects, all equally worthy of the muse. The aspirations of the Italian people after national unity, now happily fulfilled, have furnished the groundwork of 'Rome or Death!' The Commune of Paris will furnish that of the fourth and concluding canto of 'The Human Tragedy.' It is not the fault of an English poet if, reluctant to limit the range of his lyre to strains domestic or archaic, he has to cross the Channel in search of inspiration. It may be doubted if Calliope herself could turn to much account the wrangles of School Boards, the incidence of local taxation, or the payment of the American Indemnity.

The description of the campaign of Mentana, as given in the following pages, is in its broad outlines historically accurate; and if the reader should happen to know that the state of the weather or the period of the moon was not precisely such, at some particular moment, as he here finds them represented to have been, or if he should remember that more than one day actually intervened between the attack on Monte

Rotondo and the Battle of Mentana, I must ask him to believe that the disregard of literal fact in my treatment of these minor matters has not been engendered by ignorance. I think I may say, without presumption, and in order to inspire him with some little confidence in the narrative, that when I write of war, I write not at second hand, but as one who has followed it with his own steps, and seen it with his own eyes; and that in all which appertains to Italy, my sympathy has been assisted by no hasty sojourn in that seductive land, whether in the days of its affliction, during the period of its struggles, or in the present epoch of its complete regeneration. At the same time, I trust no one will suppose that my love for Italy is either prompted or accompanied by any vulgar hatred of the Church of Rome, or that I have intended, by a single line or word in the following pages, to inflame religious prejudice and rancour against a Creed for which, as having satisfied the acutest intellects, inspired the noblest actions, and been illustrated by the most perfect piety, I entertain a profound respect. The entire poem must be regarded as strictly epical and objective ; and whatever strong and even combative phrases it may contain, must be considered, not as personal utterances of the author, but rather as the reflection and representation of the feelings natural to those who were actively engaged in the attempt whose failure it records.

November 18, 1873.

ROME OR DEATH!

O THOU, the worthiest of the tuneful quire,

Muse of the pricking spear and tented field,

So long unwooed by any mortal lyre,

Wake! and to my presumptuous summons yield.

Oh! make my rhymes resound with that quick fire

Which, instant, flashes from thy stricken shield!

My verse like bounding war-horse scour the plain;

And blow thy shrilly trumpets through the strain!

A

II.

For I who first with low satiric flight,

Skimming the mortal earth, attempted wing,

Then, bolder grown, of Love's short-lived delight,

And cruel Faith's resolves, did loftier sing,

Now must ascend to empyrean height,

Where lightnings speak and deafening thunders ring,

And to the heaven of heavens of song must soar:—

Muse! help me weak—who helped the strong of yore!

III.

And thou too, lovely land! where long a guest

I happy dwelt, and whom I loved so well,

When only fair,—now not more fair than blest,—

Who breathed thy genius into Tasso's shell,

And with thy fire warmed Ariosto's breast,

Aid me! 'tis of thy hopes deferred I tell.

Smile upon me, that erst upon them smiled,—

Their all too feeble but still faithful child.

IV.

There is an isle, kissed by a smiling sea,
Where all sweet confluents meet: a thing of heaven,
A spent aërolite, that well may be
The missing sister of the starry Seven.
Celestial beauty nestles at its knee,
And in its lap is nought of earthly leaven.
'Tis girt and crowned with loveliness; its year,
Eternal summer; winter comes not near.

V.

'Tis small, as things of beauty ofttimes are,
And in a morning round it you may row,
Nor need a tedious haste your bark debar
From gliding inwards where the ripples flow
Into strange grots whose roofs are azure spar,
Whose pavements liquid silver. Mild winds blow
Around your prow, and at your keel the foam,
All gladly sporting, freshly wafts you home.

VI.

They call the island Capri;—with a name

Dulling an airy dream, just as the soul

Is clogged with body palpable;—and Fame

Hath longwhile winged the word from pole to pole.

Its human story is a tale of shame,

Of all unnatural lusts a gory scroll,

Record of what, when pomp and power agree,

Man once hath been, and man again may be.

VII.

But upon Nature's calm immortal face,

The feeble folly or enraged despair

Of paltry mortals leaves abiding trace

No more than furrow through the fields of air.

In vain would learnëd fingers point the place

Where in the isle stood ravening tyrant's lair ;

The Syrens sing around it, and the billow

To wearied limbs lends soft Lethean pillow.

ROME OR DEATH!

VIII.

Terrace and slope from shore to summit show
Of all rich climes the glad-surrendered spoil.
Here the bright olive's phantom branches glow,
There the plump fig sucks sweetness from the soil.
'Midst odorous flowers that through the Zodiac blow,
Returning tenfold to man's leisured toil,
Hesperia's fruit hangs golden. High in air,
The vine runs riot, spurning human care.

IX.

And flowers of every hue and breath abound,
Charming the sense; the burning cactus glows,
Like daisies elsewhere dappling all the ground,
And in each cleft the berried myrtle blows.
The playful lizard glides and darts around,
The elfin fireflies flicker o'er the rows
Of ripened grain. Alien to pain and wrong,
Men fill the days with dance, the nights with song.

X.

Upon a beetling cliff, eyeing the flood,

Stood one in prime of years; but there was that

In his grave gaze which told of storms withstood,

And on his brow a lofty patience sate.

His was the tranquil mien of one who would

Wrestle with fate and lay obstruction flat,

But lets the meaner ills of life go by,

Bears small shafts dumb, nor gives lewd tongues the lie.

XI.

His cheek was bronzed by ray, and wind, and wave;

His careless dress bespake a sunny land;

But his blue eye and chestnut tresses gave

Unerring tokens of a northern strand:

That strand which still begets the fair and brave,

Though there all service brave hath long been banned,

And supple Tribunes, fumbling in a hoard

Of craven gains, buy off each threatening sword.

XII.

Absorbed in luscious idleness he seemed,

Watching the languid ripples crawl to land,

As one whose bliss was deepest when he dreamed,

And who earth's beauty rather felt than scanned.

Yet oftentimes the souls all sailless deemed

By trivial gaze, with inward fires are fanned,

And neither baulked by wave nor helped by wind,

Cleave life's rough surf, when gay barks lag behind.

XIII.

When, on the pathway of the curving shore

That skirts the tideless sea, of that pure child

Who in her heart an endless sorrow bore

Sooner than grieve Madonna undefiled,

Godfrid had ta'en farewell for evermore,

Unto the Fates he breathed entreaties wild

Prompt to his hand some noble Cause to send,

Which, him befriending, he might too befriend.

XIV.

Swift was he answered. 'Neath the very sky
That roofed his restless anguish, lo! there burst,
From an uprisen People, such a cry
As ne'er was heard since heavenly Freedom first
Taught sons of men that sweeter 'tis to die
A thousand deaths, than live enslaved, accurst!
Dreamer too long, fair Italy awoke,
And with one bound her gnawing fetters broke.

XV.

The Long-expected of the Nations stood
A-tiptoe on the mountains; Morning sang
For heart of joy, and o'er the crisp blue flood
That laves soft shores, a jubilant pæan rang.
There was a stir sent through the old world's blood,
And long-hushed lyres lent dithyrambic clang.
Hope was rethroned upon her ancient seat,
And pining peoples came and kissed her feet.

XVI.

The soaring dream of poets in their graves ;
The creed by patriot martyrs, as they smiled,
Clutched like a cross, when Custom's ready slaves
Around their flesh the flaming faggots piled :
Dawn seen in durance dim of midnight caves
By sightless eyes of souls waxed weird and wild ;—
All now had burgeoned, and from sea to sea,
From shore to summit, Italy was free !

XVII.

No more 'midst dank lagunes and oozing walls,
Echoing to silence, Venice crouched and wept ;
A glow was on her waters ; to her halls
The lustrous glamour of gay eld had crept.
Last of the dull Barbarian's dainty thralls
To feel her limbs, up to her feet she leapt,
Clasping her Lombard brother by the hand,
Whilst throbs of welcome trembled through the Land.

XVIII.

For, ere her woes had moved the heart of ruth,
Day on her lone divided kindred broke.
The bright Parthenope renewed her youth,
And lithe Etruria slipped the tyrant's yoke.
Umbria shook off the gnawing church-wolf's tooth,
And, happy once again, Campania woke;
And round rent Savoy's Cross as hot they pressed,
Italia clasped her children to her breast.

XIX.

All—all—save one! Rome still in fetters lay,
Writhing beneath the hierarch's heavy heel;
The eldest-born of all that bright array,
From franchised kith cut off by warding steel.
For fitful Gaul, whose trumpets first did bray
Salvation o'er the hill-tops, feebly leal
To its own dream, from all high quests had ceased,
Playing scorned gaoler to a trembling priest!

XX.

And all the world looked on with gaze of stone,
Cold or approving; for the days were ill.
Some said the Altar propped the sceptic Throne,
And, twin at birth, they must be coupled still;
Some, that no more Christ's Godhead could be shown,
Save Peter's sword chastised the infidel;
And some, that Italy e'en now was blest
All overmuch, and Europe wanted rest.

XXI.

So in the gyves by tonsured tyrants wrought
Rome still lay languishing, nor spake for woe,
But only with pale eyes her kin besought
To watch the hour to smite her keeper low.
Therefore they waited; for was worse than nought
Their own reproachful freedom, whilst the blow
Unstruck remained, and in the obscene dust
Their purest blood fed Gaul's vainglorious lust.

XXII.

So every eye and heart were turned to Rome,
And hands were sworn to vengeance. Maidens thrust
Their lovers from them, spurning peaceful home
Whilst blades still crouched in scabbards, lolled in rust.
Round their brown limbs as plashed the purple must,
Or with the share they ploughed the wavy loam,
All sang of Rome : " Rome, Rome shall yet be ours !
Sleep, Tyrants, sleep ! we count the ripening hours."

XXIII.

The sickle's arm caressed the lissom corn,
To strains that throbbed of Rome ; the blade which pruned
The straggling elm or lopped the truant thorn,
At each brave stroke to songs of Rome was tuned.
The shepherd boy upon the hills forlorn,
When his tired flock in sweet siesta swooned,
On his rude reed piped plaintively of Rome,
And, tiny patriot, heaved a sigh for home.

XXIV.

The winds that shrilled through each adventurous shroud

That skimmed the Tyrrhene sea, rang loud of Rome ;

To songs of Rome were timed the arms that bowed

O'er Hadria's oar or clave Liguria's foam.

The quarry's hollow bosom echoed loud

The self-same notes ; and where the chamois clomb

In fancied fastness, 'twas that ditty sweet,—

Sweet if yet sad,—that scared its flying feet.

XXV.

Round the warm hearth or under chilly stars

Did men and women gather, talking low ;

And as the stalwart grimly stroked their scars,

Bold striplings murmured, "We, too, sure shall go ? "

Now every brawny babe was gat of Mars,

And suckled by a she-wolf ; bred to grow

To god-like heights by heavenly blood impelled,

And rear a Rome e'en brighter than of eld.

XXVI.

But they who ruled the land since Death had dragged

Down to his greedy cave the daring mind

That staked, to swell, its fortunes, sate all gagged,

And in the swathes of policy confined.

With halting gait the would-be leaders lagged

Behind the led, and feebly watched the wind,

Nursing a craven hope that Fortune's wheel

Would drop the prize they feared to snatch by steel.

XXVII.

So to the rocky home of him who still

Bore Aspromonte's bullet in his flesh,

All hopes were strained, that soon his chafing will

Would flash the blade and flaunt the flag afresh ;

That he, their Cincinnatus, who did till

Idly the niggard soil, would rend the mesh

The alien round them wove, and, long-implored,

Beat out at last his ploughshare to a sword.

XXVIII.

With Italy's flowing fortunes Godfrid's sword,
By Victory's wave upborne, had ridden still :
Fleshed on that day when first the Austrian horde
Was swept from Lombard plain, nor sheathed until
The unclean Bourbon monster lay and roared,
Like old Typhœus crushed 'neath Ischia's hill ;
And from Romagna's gangrened flesh and worn
Amortized limbs, were priest-clinched shackles torn.

XXIX.

Then came that chilling pause, when though from peak
Of Apennine and Alp to dimpling wave,
The glow of Freedom mantled o'er the cheek
Of the fair land, in shadow of the grave
Rome grovelled mute, and Venice, pale and weak,
Sobbed 'neath her Teuton ravisher,—lovely slave,
Who, reared at Liberty's maternal knee,
Yearned for the pure embraces of the free.

XXX.

Even to her, deliverance came at last,

Yet not in the sweet guise brave men had dreamed.

Though Italy aside the scabbard cast,

Upon her blade no ray of victory gleamed.

But 'mong the realms by force and fraud amassed,

Whilst rival robbers each from other schemed

To filch a province for his own domains,

Then Venice seized the hour, and slipped her chains.

XXXI.

Not on Custozza's baneful field, but where

Trent cleaves Tyrolean Alp, had Godfrid fought,

And, when the sword was sheathed, within this fair

Famed isle, at once a home and watch-tower sought,

Waiting for day to dawn on Rome's despair ;

And hither oft would come, and, steeped in thought

And sunshine, silent watch from Capri's brow

The soft sea lave its feet, even as now.

XXXII.

But ever and anon he cast a look
To-day towards where among the vines was seen
A girl, in brilliant dyes arrayed, which took
E'en gaudier splendour from surrounding green.
The tangled leaves and tendrils did she hook
Deftly around her kirtle's crimson sheen ;
With crimson was her brimming boddice dight,
And snow-white kerchief hid her charms from sight.

XXXIII.

Her body was of glorious make ; her limbs
Vaunted the strain of that Olympian line,
Reared upon earth, as sung in deathless hymns,
When mortal mould was filled with juice divine.
The mist of Time the glowing story dims,
But bear me witness, ye Immortal Nine !
That Jove's stout stock still lingers in the isle,
And Venus yet in daughters fair doth smile.

B

XXXIV.

Her skin was lustrous as the ripening grape,

And, like the grape's, the sanguine flesh beamed through ;

Her eyes could match the olive's dainty shape,

And all outshone its dark and burnished hue.

Twisted in coils above the massive nape,

Her classic hair grand memories did renew,

Back from her brow, free from fantastic wiles,

Rippling like Ocean, when dark Ocean smiles.

XXXV.

She seemed a bright embodiment of one

Of those too marble visions that were lent

To Grecian eyes ere Art's brief race was run,

Wherein grace, strength, and beauty all were blent:

A statue stirred to motion ; by the sun

All breathing made for mortal ravishment;

A dream with flesh endued; a chiselled thought,

Catching warm being from the hand that wrought.

ROME OR DEATH!

XXXVI.

She was not learnëd in that bookish lore
Which men call knowledge; but her arms could ply
In the stiff surge withal a valorous oar,
And her quick hands make the frail shuttle fly.
It was her fingers wove the dress she wore,
What time the Night held more than half the sky;
And when the days were long, from dawn to close
Still would she climb, nor ever crave repose.

XXXVII.

And yet she was a woman,—gently framed
For loving purposes. The murderous snare
She never set, nor barrel deadly-aimed
At bird or beast would she consent to bear.
E'en in the fishers' net her hands disclaimed
All helpful service; but when none were there,
Oft she disported 'mong the timorous tribe,
Her glorious breasts ploughing the brine aside.

XXXVIII.

The womb that bore her, like a tree with fruit
Too rich and rare, had perished with her birth;
And, ere she lisped, her sire's fond lips grew mute
For aye, and she was left alone on earth.
No, not alone; for every native lute
Was tuned to glad her little ears with mirth;
And now along the mainland, many a mile,
Men sang the lovely Orphan of the Isle.

XXXIX.

She played on no rare instrument or rude,
Her homely fingers knew no dainty trick;
But oh! her voice with cunning was imbued
To soothe the soul or cheat the spirit sick.
Hear her, e'en now, in fancied solitude,
As slow she moves among the vineyard thick,
Singing a song of Liberty, to pierce
Fate's dullard ears, and soften tyrants fierce!

XL.

"Miriam!" he called; but ere the word was blown

Athwart the leafy distance to her ear,

The softly-dying strain again had grown

To silvery volume, sweet but piercing clear.

Enthralled, he listened to each melting tone,

Each stirring note, till both did disappear

In the blue air, then "Miriam!" called once more.

"I come," she cried, and straight towards him bore.

XLI.

In either hand a bunch of grapes she held:

The left were garnet, opal were the right;

Clustering and tapering, full-veined, sunshine-swelled,

They would have filled Dionysus with delight;

One of whose Charities of early eld

She seemed, with every genial grace bedight;

That gentle Triad who the innocent earth

Girdled with music, modesty, and mirth.

XLII.

And as she came anear, the juicy bells

She merrily held and dangled in his face.

"Eat, eat of these; for old tradition tells

That they the sombre soul's worst clouds can chase."

Then with that frank simplicity which dwells

Alone in unsophisticated grace,

She added soft, "Accept the simple cheer,

My tithe to him who preaches all the year."

XLIII.

His grave set face thawed to a sunny smile,

For well he seized the maiden's arch intent.

She was as strange to wrong, as free from guile,

As flower on stalk or singing bird unpent.

But even in that small and simple isle

Were pitfalls for the unwary; and he lent

A chiding voice at times to heedless feet,

When timid tongues in whispers sought retreat.

XLIV.

"Thanks for my tithe, dear Miriam," he said ;
"Perchance it is a trifle overdue ;
But you do pay me interest instead :—
I cross old scores, and we commence anew.
'Tis fortunate you came ; for in my head
There runs another sermon. Nay, 'tis true,
And I *will* preach it. Come, be patient, dear !
See, there are only you, and I, and waves, to hear."

XLV.

"Suppose,"—and on the rocky ledge that lay
Between them and the leap to death below,
He spread the glowing gifts,—"suppose that they
Who coaxed the ardent generous vine to throw
Its tendrils out, and to the ripening ray
Of sunny heaven its swelling beads to show,
When they were ripe and bursting, even as now,
Should turn away, and leave them on the bough ?—

XLVI.

" Leave them to shrink and wizen in the wind,

For the hot sun that fostered root and stem,

To scorch their moist pulp, burn their cooling rind,

And all the airs of heaven to rifle them,

Though caves meanwhile with empty vats were lined,

And throats as dry as some trite apophthegm?

Suppose that this should happen—here—to-day—

Here, here in Capri—what would Miriam say?"

XLVII.

" Why, that the folks were mad. But there's no fear.

Your parable lacks truth. Nay, look around!

The joyous Vintage' purple hours are near,

And wine-stirred feet ere long shall beat the ground.

They come, they come, the merry band! I hear

Our light-long toil in songs of plenty drowned;

We wreathe our brows with vine-leaves, and we sing,

Whilst cape and creek with laughing echoes ring."

XLVIII.

"Right merrily answered, Miriam, and right true.

Yet harken to me, dear! There is a God,

To whom the God of Wine's but a deity new,

A thing of yesterday, a faun, a clod,

A tipsy nothing! Nay, I warrant you,

That long ere Bacchus breathed into the sod

The secret of the grape, the God of Love

Owned this fair world and shared the world above.

XLIX.

"Yes, wine is good; it thaws the ice-bound breast,

And pawing Fancy's fairy steeds unchains,

Rouses the torpid soul from churlish rest,

With floods of summer flushing wintry veins.

'Tis wine that flutters the poet in his nest,

Plumes his light wing and warms his liquid strains,

Curtails long nights, and hath the charm to steep

Outwearied limbs in deep undreaming sleep.

L.

" Yes, wine is good, but Love is better still;

For it assails the pulses of the heart

With swift yet soft suffusions. Love doth fill

Life's vacant hollows, worse than any smart,

With pleasant tumults, surging joys that thrill

The silent soul to music. 'Tis an art

Which maketh poets of us all ; we sing

Like Sappho's self, when Love once tunes the string.

LI.

" Its children are delicious dreams, that haunt

The brain awake or sleeping ; its bright lures

Alone confer the ecstasy they vaunt,

The one divine delirium that endures.

On Love's light step attend no shadows gaunt,

And all its own sweet wounds its sweet self cures.

It fans but feeds the warmly-glowing flesh,

And slakes the thirst it still creates afresh.

LII.

" But Love, like these fair tokens of the vine,

Hath, too, its times and seasons. First, its spring ;

Days of sweet doubts and fear, when smiles like thine,

Daintier than tendrils, to the heart-strings cling.

Next, its enticing summer, when the bine

Of mounting hope brave leaves abroad doth fling,

And softly-swelling vows, Love's crowning gift,

Fed by its life-blood, peep through each green rift.

LIII.

" Then, last of all, Love's luscious autumn time,

When all its dreams are ripened. Fear hath fled.

No more the heart Suspicion's chilling rime,

Or blight of scorching Jealousy, need dread.

Love's hour is here ; Love's vintage-bells may chime,

And Love's festoons be wreathed round board and bed.

He reels with ripeness: press his sweetness out,

Whilst Hymen's songs the hills and valleys shout !

LIV.

"But haply should we scorn Love's full desires,
Nor all its teeming wealth make haste to press,
Oh, then it shrivels of its own spurned fires,
And all its goodly promise perishes.
Then shall no love-cup cheat the toil that tires,
Nor care be chased by wedlock's staunch caress.
Yes, mad indeed, we have squandered all our store,
The harvest of our youth, which comes no more.

LV.

"Ah! heed me, heed me, Miriam! for I speak
A parable that lacks nor truth nor aim.
Answer me truly: have I 'far to seek
To point the moral that I scarce need name?
Do I not read in rosy-glowing cheek,
In palpitating veins, in eye aflame,
Love in your heart would build himself a nest,
If you would only house that gentle guest?

LVI.

"Why, why repel him, why, indeed, delay,

Since he doth come in so mature a guise?

Look down; 'tis Gilbert's bark that cleaves the spray

Far at our feet, his arm the oar that plies.

What if Time's touch hath flecked his beard with grey,

It veils a breast more steadfast and more wise.

Ah! Youth in man is fickle! Not the fire

That warms the hearth, is fed on green desire.

LVII.

"Ere I the golden pastures of my youth

Had yet quite left behind, I met with one,

Whose gentleness might well have moved the ruth

Of Fate itself, but was by Fate undone.

One whom—well, one who loved me; for, in sooth,

My heart had yet not opened to the sun,

Though in the half-closed bud there lurked a growth

Of sweet and bitter, fatal to us both.

LVIII.

" So young and yielding ! I, so young and blind,

And poor in all that men, alas ! call wealth,

In which they still their happiness would find.

Often we met, though never once by stealth :

We were as open as the sun or wind ;

For in the heyday of our life and health,

With careless feet and heedless hearts we go

Along the yawning precipice of woe.

LIX.

" Gilbert I knew not then, though in the crowd

His name had heard, as one whom worldlings rate

Half as a god, since veiled in golden cloud.

Whom shall I blame ?   Not him—not her—but Fate,

And that vile splendour which is poor Love's shroud,

And whose pomp leaves the heart still desolate.

They broke no human law, and they were wed :—

Woman to man—the living to the dead !

LX.

"Nay, look not so! The unsurrendering grave
Holds all that was of her. She is at rest.
In these poor arms her last sad sob she gave.
I sought her not. Against my guiltless breast
'Twas destiny her helmless soul that drave
And whelmed her drifting life. Well—death was best.
And now she bears, from where the saints look down,
The virgin's palm, and wears the martyr's crown.

LXI.

'Twas on the very eve of that great day
When Freedom dawned, I met her, in despair,
In Florence, where he fever-stricken lay.
Sheathing my sword, I seconded her care,
And dragged him back to life. To our dismay,
Straight then she sickened; and nor skill nor prayer
Availed us aught. Science no help could give,
But only wondered why she would not live.

LXII.

"There is no name for that of which she died,
Unless we call it weariness of heart,
Which still doth kill, though mortals oft deride
Its power, and 'gainst its poison boast their art.
I to the last stayed, helpful, by her side,
Bearing, as best I might, my grievous part,
Since Gilbert held me.   Still I think he guessed
Before she died, what ne'er could be confessed!

LXIII.

"She neither wronged, and she was wronged by both.
But she so gentle was, that this I know—
She both will have forgiven.   Ah! men are loth
To pay the debt to penitence they owe,
And love's light vows contrast with wedlock's troth,
To screen their own misdoing, and the woe
On others they inflict.   Both—both—I say,
Wronged her, and owned it when she lifeless lay.

LXIV.

"Together both did bear her to the grave,
Together mourned. Gilbert, too noble far,
To wrong her, dead, all but himself forgave,
And, by my side, following that wind of war
Which blowing up from Freedom's freshening wave,
Routed the clouds that hid thy country's star,
Sought, even as I, in worthy deeds to gain
Pardon for fault, oblivion for pain.

LXV.

"He is a noble gentleman and true,
Whom sorrow hath made sage. He loves you, dear,
And still will love you when no more the dew
Of sunny morn shall in your cheeks appear.
I am no messenger; no more than you,
Hath he confessed his secret to my ear.
But Love is a silent babbler, and I need
No words of his or yours, your hearts to read.

C

LXVI.

"Nor can you plead him alien in blood,
For he hath made your country's cause his own.
Have I not seen him 'midst the sanguine flood
Through which she waded to her rightful throne,
And by the bayonet's threat and cannon's thud
Marked his tame port of peace heroic grown?
And when we deemed the hour to do or die
For Rome had struck, did not his soul reply?

LXVII.

"Oh! hapless Aspromonte! Cursëd field,
And all too bitter hill! I saw him there,
His veins consumed with rage, but sword congealed,
Since our hurt chieftain bade us all forbear.
And do you doubt that when the hour hath pealed,
Rousing our baffled lion from his lair,
He too will fly from this delicious foam,
To fight—who knows? perhaps to fall—for Rome?"

LXVIII.

"O yes," she answered, glowing as she spake,

His last words flushing her dark cheeks with fire,

"I know that he would die for Italy's sake,

And that is why—I swear it by my sire,

My mother's sacred dust, my country's ache—

I yet will give him all his soul's desire!

Thou art my more than brother ; he shall be

Second to none—not, Godfrid, e'en to thee!

LXIX.

"Yet list to me in turn, albeit I sound

Beggar in speech that doth enrich your tongue.

I said but now that none so mad were found,

Who, when these clusters full to bursting hung

From stalk and stem, and o'er the happy ground

From tree to tree in drooping garlands swung,

Would scorn the sweet pulp wrapped in beaming rind,

And leave the jocund juice to feed the wind.

LXX.

"But see! Our vintage dawns. Yet do you doubt,
That if to-morrow, though brave loins were girt,
Brisk sleeves knit up, our baskets spread about,
The scoured vats all agape for wine to spirt
Down their huge throats, we heard a sudden shout
Of 'Rome or Death!' and saw the brave red shirt
Flame like a beacon—we should, one and all,
Leave vat, leave vine, responsive to the call?

LXXI.

"Should we not quit the harvest of the year,
To gather in the harvest of all time?
He—you—yes I—leave grape and grain, nor fear
To reap 'mid thirst and want a store sublime?
Swords were our sickles then; the milk-white steer
No more with purple loads our slopes would climb;
Its peaceful flanks 'neath warlike wains would foam,
Splashed with their blood who barred the path to Rome!

LXXII.

" Bear with me then, I pray, my brother kind,

And bid him bear awhile whose love I prize.

So long as the Priest-King my kith doth bind

In Peter's chains,—well, Rome hath all my sighs !

I have no heart for tenderness, no mind

For pillowed sweets, no ear for baby cries.

Oh ! I should blush if Conflict's thrilling noise

Should reach me, cooing over selfish joys ! "

LXXIII.

She ceased ; and he was silent in his soul,

Drinking her noble rhetoric.   But whilst each

Watched mute the creamy ripples landwards roll,

Up the rude path that zigzagged from the beach,

A bright-eyed urchin, with a fluttering scroll,

Skipping and tumbling came,—too blown for speech ;

His pretty cheeks with speed-drops all aglow,

And tangled curls, left in the breeze to blow.

LXXIV.

Hearing the swift step, Godfrid turned his head,

And quick the little Mercury, pressed for breath,

Thrust in his hand the scroll, then, panting, said,

"Read—read! the game's afoot of 'Rome or Death!'

See! Garibaldi from his isle hath sped,

And the whole land to join him hasteneth.

All Naples is astir; and look! they write,

This time the King will cheer, not foil, the fight."

LXXV.

And as he spake, and Godfrid scanned the scroll,

And saw that he spake true, again the shout

Of "Rome or Death!" burst on his startled soul.

And half-way down to wave, where jutted out

From skeleton crag a green and grassy mole,

Down-peering spied they Gilbert, waving about

A blood-red flag, and loud with lusty breath

Crying, "Come! Godfrid! Miriam! Rome or Death!"

LXXVI.

As swift as light, Miriam round Godfrid's neck

Flung wild her arms, and all as quickly loosed;

Then, without more ado or ever a check,

Down the steep path they ran, like streams unsluiced:

So fast, that soon the summits were a speck

Where late they stood,—the sea-bird's stormy roost.

And audibly now they heard the billows bound,

Which there had seemed to die without a sound.

LXXVII.

And, ever as they sped, waxed loud and oft

The cry, "Rome, Rome or Death!" Each feathery holt,

Each sinuous down, each peak that pricked aloft,

Flung back the words, echoing the grand revolt.

And swift from vineyard, terrace, garden, croft,

As, straight on lightning, swoops the thunderbolt,

Flashed all the folk, in gathering crowd and roar,

And with one pulse descending to the shore.

LXXVIII.

As snows on heights of Apennine that long,
Silenced by Winter's iron hand, have lain,
When Spring weeps smiling tears, burst icy thong,
And, melting into music, bound amain
This way and that, through thousand channels throng,
Snatching each track that leads them to the plain,
Nor till their mad erratic race is o'er,
In the broad valley's bosom blend once more;

LXXIX.

E'en so the people of that mountain home,
By frosty fetters longwhile hushed and cooped,
Hearing the vernal voice call from the foam,
Straight from their rock-set thresholds wildly trooped,
Streaming adown where scarce the goatherd clomb,
And leaping whence the curved-clawed falcon swooped;
A swift and separate trackway scoured by each,
Until all met and mingled at the beach.

LXXX.

Thither too, whooping loud, thronged untamed boys,
Bare-browed, bare-breasted, gemmed with eager eyes,
With rapid questions heightening all the noise,
Then breaking off, nor waiting for replies.
And glowing maids were there, full ripe for joys
Not found in battle: Goddesses in size,
With massive pitchers on their heads, at ease
Standing like stalwart Caryatides;

LXXXI.

Nor moving lip, but with full gaze intent
On lovers who but yesternight did woo,
And now no more coined words of blandishment,
But arched their blades, and felt the edge was true.
'Twixt their fair serried shoulders forwards leant,
With craning necks and faces sharp to view,
Low-chattering crones, wailing the lonely lot
Of these thus left, who heard but heeded not.

LXXXII.

And, last of all, grave matrons joined the throng,

Babes upon arm, that only lisped as yet

The words of Rome and mother;—grave and strong,

With thoughtful brows, but eyelids all unwet:

Whilst 'mong the crowd bent greybeards hobbled along,

Blessing the Lord that ere their sun had set,

They had seen this day; yet railing half at Fate,

That sent salvation, for their aid too late.

LXXXIII.

Then high debate arose who first should go,

Who linger last, and who at home must stay.

Some, fledged with shafts of death from tip to toe,

Vowed none should snatch or turn them from the fray;

Some could a rusty matchlock only show,

And some a rough-edged bill-hook but display;

These from the hearth had snatched up smouldering brands,

Whilst those had brawny thews but empty hands.

LXXXIV.

But once upon the mainland, arms would swift

For all be found. And, as they said, there came

Women and girls with many a farewell gift :

Strings of fat quails for which the isle hath fame,

And figs distilling honey through each rift

Of their moist rinds ; bread, worthy sure to name

E'en as to give ; huge bunches from the vine

All newly plucked ; and flasks of rosy wine.

LXXXV.

Meanwhile from where, under the frowning cliff,

In days gone by long waves had worn a cave,

Godfrid and Gilbert dragged a gallant skiff,

And the sharp keel straight through the shingle drave.

A moment at the sand-bar halting stiff,

It heeled, then lurched ; and as it touched the wave,

The waters rose to take it, and it lay

Trembling with gladness on the circling spray.

LXXXVI.

Her face superb lit by a flashing smile,

Into the boat first Miriam lightly stepped;

Two sinewy youths, the pick of all the isle,

Followed, and briskly to their places leapt;

Then Gilbert, and last Godfrid. Poised awhile,

Down swooped the oars, and then away they swept:

Whilst all the folk cried after them, " Death or Rome !

Swift speed your bark ! we follow in its foam."

LXXXVII.

Then like to her who erst, when Egypt's host

Pursued God's people and the Red Sea ford

Opened and closed upon the heathen boast,

Snatched timbrel up and magnified the Lord;

So Miriam now, as further fled the coast,

In jubilant song her swelling soul outpoured,

And 'twixt the bright blue sky and deep blue main,

In the blue air rang out this sounding strain !

I.

Through scarred Chiusa's choked ravine
  Fierce-foaming Dora flows,
Where hearts are free and fearless e'en
  As its own suckling snows.
Past Casentino's fruitful vale
  See smiling Arno glide,
On where fair Florence, famed in tale,
  Glows like a youthful bride.
'Mong green Venafro's olive slopes
  Volturno twists and winds,
And, laughing, triples all the hopes
  Of Capua's happy hinds.
'Tis only Tiber—Tiber—crawls,
  Sullen from swamp to sea.
Awake, ye deaf! Arise, ye thralls!
Country cries, Freedom calls;
And by all the Gods, maugre all the Gauls,
  O Italy, my Italy,
  Thou shalt be one and free!

2.

The Lombard, stayed by no man's frown,
  Treads his well-watered fields,
And shakes the nutty harvest down
  From Como's waving wealds.
Singing till dusk, with vacant breast,
  Love-ditties o'er and o'er,
The easy Tuscan drops to rest
  Amid his ample store.
For teeming herds and fleecy flocks
  The Apulian spurns the share ;
Moist swathes, plump fruits, and full-eared shocks,
  Crown the Campanian's care.
Why then alone round Rome's wide walls
  Should barren deserts be ?
Snatch blade and brand, O famished thralls !
Country cries, Freedom calls ;
And by all the Gods, maugre all the Gauls,
  Fair Italy, proud Italy,
  Thou must be one and free !

3.

Shorn of its shackles, Venice feels

   The vulture's·beak no more,

And lightly speed the unclogged keels

   Along the Oscan shore.

His sleek-skinned team and swaying pole

   The free Æmilian drives ;

Safe sows and reaps the Romagnole,

   Loosed from the shaveling's gyves.

Vesuvius answers Ætna's fires,

   Mainland and isle join hands,

And men and maids in joyous choirs

   Dance on Sicilian sands.

What! And shall peal in Rome's great halls

   No rite of pride or glee ?

Up from your knees, ye priest-crushed thralls !

Country cries, Freedom calls ;

And by all the Gods, maugre all the Gauls,

   Dear Italy, grand Italy,

     Thou wilt be one and free !

LXXXVIII.

Thus rippling died the note o'er broad blue bay,

Now smooth as cheek of childhood. Not a speck

Of foam or surf, save as they clave their way,

Broke the expanse from headland neck to neck.

Faster they seemed to spurn the following spray,

Than mortal keel which winds and waters check,

And, spite the rhythmic strokes doughtily given,

On to the mainland rather drawn than driven.

LXXXIX.

Now on the left rough Massa rose to view,

Now soft Sorrento. Then they swept along

Past populous shores where vine-veiled ashes strew

Cities which echoed once to dance and song.

Now on the right dark.Ischia flecked the blue,

Where Nature's penitent hand smooths ancient wrong;

And soon the mighty mountain 'gan to loom,

That floods with streams of death its fiery womb.

XC.

Till close behind them now they caught the hum
Of many voices, and the rising roar
Of noisy Naples, mingled with the strum
And twang of sharp guitar along the shore.
A moment more, and with the cry "We come,"
Bare-legged and Phrygian-capped, upon them bore
A rush of boatmen, voluble of speech,
Who drew the light skiff swiftly up the beach.

XCI.

Then out they sprang,—first Miriam, Gilbert next,
Last Godfrid,—and the eager host pressed round ;
Rude fishermen, hoarse women half unsexed,
And rude sea-urchins frisking o'er the ground.
Each with chaotic shouts their ears perplexed,
Questions and answers in the hubbub drowned,
O'er which there surged alone, as springs the foam
Above loud waves, the cry of "Death or Rome !"

D

XCII.

But as they thrust the phrensied crowd aside,

And pushed on to the city's beating heart,

At every step their hopes grew verified,

And warlike omens bade their doubts depart.

Men, new in arms, gathering from far and wide,

Made but a martial muster-ground the mart.

Churches were changed to barracks; and the cars

Of Ceres' self were given up to Mars.

XCIII.

The .very streets volcanic seemed and roared

Like Somma's fiery self, and seething flowed

With streams of living lava, ever poured

Hot from the City's innermost abode.

And, over all, ever and anon there soared

Convulsive detonations, such as goad

To agony of madness feet that fly

Wavewards, when roused Vesuvius shells the sky !

XCIV.

And then night fell, and fairy lamps shone out
From balcony and lattice. High in air,
Gay gonfalons were lightly blown about,
And at the windows crowded faces fair.
On the choked pavement shrill-lunged lads did shout
The great news forth, and in the shining square,
Hard by the Palace, flushed with jets of light,
Men sate in groups and conned the coming fight.

XCV.

Just ere the hour drew near for lamps to fade
And all the world to fall away to rest,
Far up Toledo shrilling trumpets brayed.
Straight at the sound, thither all footsteps pressed,
And, as if ranged for battle's stern parade,
Formed in deep files and long lines drawn abreast,
And, close in phalanx packed, with ringing cheer,
"Viva Italia! Evviva!" rent the ear.

XCVI.

Rang out once more the clarion's cleaving blare,

And rudely rumbled hollow-bowelled drum ;

Then strains of martial music stormed the air,

And away they strode, steps sounding but lips dumb.

But at the windows, still, cheered voices fair,

And waved white kerchiefs gallantly ; while some

Sweet flowers drew forth from bosoms yet more sweet,

And showered them down to kiss the tramping feet.

XCVII.

When, with a sudden and barbaric clang,

The strong soft music snapped, the phalanxed crowd

Then lifted up their voices all, and sang

In unison a chorus long and loud.

It was a strain to scare the despot's fang,

And wake the sleeping patriot in his shroud ;

And, as it died, again the bellowing cry,

" Viva Italia ! Evviva !" stunned the sky.

XCVIII.

Then midnight dropped, and all the city was still.
Inarime lay darkling on the sea ;
Faint spikes of flame tipped Somma's murky hill,
And on the shore the waves died silently.
The fabled fields the Mantuan's wizard quill
Steeps in undying glamour, seemed to be
Once more Elysian, and the night-winds lay
Cradled on Baiæ's ruin-pebbled bay.

XCIX.

Bewitching land!   How oft, 'mid cold grey skies,
Mist-blurred horizons, landscapes chilled with rime,
Have I not yearned with long-forbidden eyes
For one more vision of your sunny clime!
Oh! more than e'en the hart e'er pants and sighs
For the delicious waterbrooks, I climb
The heights of beckoning hope, and from afar
Strain to behold you, even as you are!

C.

For in my boyhood, with no boy's disdain,
I scanned the classic tale. The Sibyl's cave,
Cumæ's dread grot, the charred Phlegræan plain,
Avernus' lethal lake, and wave-washed grave,
Where, silent long, clarion and oar have lain
That helped Æneas o'er the Tyrrhene wave,—
These, ere I touched them verily, were the goal
Of my mind's eye, and fired my tender soul.

CI.

Came youth, and by thy haunted strand I strayed,
Alone, yet not an exile, save as those
Who, since they think not with their kind, are made
To feel their loneliness, and nursed my woes
In thy soft smiles; and now again, when weighed
With too much ill, the sad old yearning grows
For thy bright shores, and, wearied with life's gloom,
To seek—what Virgil found—a sunny tomb!

CII.

Gay broke the morn, and now along the land,

On with the day the joyous tidings grew;

Passed the fleet spray round Spartivento's strand,

And raced with Manfredonia's billows blue.

Swifter than falcon by Libeccio fanned,

All up the long-backed Apennine it flew,

And, lithe as mists by sunrise skywards drawn,

Scaled Alpine heights and, bright, proclaimed the dawn.

CIII.

It brought the lilies out in Florence fair,

Flooded with life Bologna's grim arcades,

Fluttered the doves in Venice' marble square,

Filled Milan's thrifty streets with generous blades.

Perugia's griffin laid his talons bare,

And lions leaped from Padua's learnèd shades;

Whilst Turin's generous beast, swift at the sound,

Lowered his horned front, and, pawing, shook the ground.

CIV.

In many a busy street swart sons of toil,

Humming their ditties full in mid-day glare,

As with quick hands they mixed the glutinous soil,

Or, perched on dizzying scaffolds high in air,

Laid straight the stone or chipped the quaint gurgoyle,

Or with sharp chisel carved the cornice fair,

Smote by the cry, suspended stroke and song,

And swarmed below to swell the frantic throng.

CV.

They left the half-mixed mortar where it lay,

Flung down the rule, the trowel cast aside,

Whilst rope and pulley o'er the public way

All idly hung, unfreighted and unplied.

In suburbs, long with noise of labour gay,

Sound of reverberating hammer died.

The stern assessor at the Gate his dues

For once forgot, and rushed to glean the news.

CVI.

Good-natured mimes, conning their coming parts,
Flooding with fabled tears their facile eyes,
Loading with fancied love-throes their soft hearts,
Or swelling out their limbs to kingly size,
With well-aped mien defying tyrants' smarts,
Swift at the sound doffed feeble masks and lies,
Grasped genuine swords, mock patriots no more,
Nor played with blood, who soon should taste of gore.

CVII.

They too who still nooks keep 'mid city's bray,
Moulding their plastic dreams, or move among
Colours that live beyond life's little day,
Scared by the tumult, to their windows sprung,
Then kissed their models sweet, and rushed away;
Leaving the tints unfinished fancy flung,
Or the dim forms, dawning through marble shell,
Till their return in solitude to dwell.

CVIII.

Ah! will they e'er return? Or must those fair
But only half-fledged shapes lie wombed for aye,
Fast in their embryonic limbo there,
Like unbaptisëd innocents doomed to stay
In a dim purgatory, barred to prayer,
Denied the dark, denied the light of day;
Whilst they who should have lent them life and breath,
Float down the stream of unreturning Death?

CIX.

Ah! *will* they e'er return? They did not ask,
But thronged unheeding to the feast of steel,
Swift as glad schoolboys sally from their task,
And gay as gallant, when the joy-bells peal,
Strides to his bridal, or with lowered casque
To mimic tourney plies the rowelled heel.
Pledged they not " Rome or Death!"? And they that try
Immortal deeds, can scarcely fear to die.

CX.

Nor these alone, but hearts of humbler strain,
Rose to the heights of valour.   Hands that wield
The craven instruments of feeble gain,
Clamoured for weapons of the priceless field ;
Whilst noble brows no longer looked disdain
On villain thews that brandished sword and shield.
All men were foster-brothers now, and pressed
A glorious kinship from their country's breast.

CXI.

Far off upon the mountain's marble side,
In rough-hewn amphitheatres whose bold tiers,
Scaling the sky, white crowned with blue, defied
With unprotected front the storms of years,—
Round huge blocks coiling nervous ropes tight-tied,
Or urging sinewy bullocks with goads and jeers,
Carrara's sun-scorched toilers, at the sound
Unwonted, paused, and wildly stared around.

CXII.

'Twas louder, deeper, longer than the roar

That rocks and rends the giant-bowelled hills,

When quarrying blast tears down the mountain hoar,

And the scarred gorge with echoing thunder fills.

Hark, how beyond where wreaths sulphureous soar,

It rings, and rises, and the welkin thrills,

And with resounding summons seeks and calls

For hands like theirs to breach Rome's crumbling walls !

CXIII.

Steadying with brawny thews through rich brown soil

The unwieldy antique plough that Rhea's son

Drave round his regal Palatine, lusty swains

The challenge caught, and, as at signal gun,

Left the unfinished furrow ; left their wains

Standing half-piled ; left their sleek oxen dun ;

Left pretty wife, smooth babe, and clambering boy,

Nor stopped to snatch one desultory joy.

CXIV.

Here had the purple vintage just begun,
Here it was drawing to its golden close;
Whilst there beyond, its bright mid-course was run,
Gay figures glinting 'mong the verdant rows.
Voice upon voice was singing in the sun
The virtues of the vine that routs our woes,
Spurs bashful youth with warmly bold desires,
And thaws the virgin's veins with subtle fires.

CXV.

When lo! above the rhythmical ebb and swell
Of genial hymn, and chorus lustily cried,
Surged one strong note, loud as that brave old bell
With which Capponi Charles's threat defied.
There was no ear so dull but knew it well,
No lip so slow but "Rome or Death!" replied;
No heart so sordid, but the crowning store
Of the year's toil enslaved its care no more.

CXVI.

They left the long unstrung festoons half-stripped,
The tall deep crates half-filled, the vats unpressed,
In the first trough their hands empurpled dipped,
Doffed work-day gear, and called for gay red vest;
Then, with brief, brave farewells, away they tripped,
Eager as fledglings from forsaken nest,
Whilst not one hand was raised to bid them stay,
One tear let fall to clog them on their way.

CXVII.

No need had they to ask what path was theirs,
More than the runnels from the mountain's brow
'Mong myriad streams, or in a flight of stares
Vanguard or rearguard whither it shall plough
The airy track, which wing to wing declares.
For every hamlet was a beacon now,
And each man's tongue a tocsin. Does its way
The tide or tempest doubt? No more did they.

CXVIII.

True as the needle to the northern pole,

All eyes were set towards Rome, and there abode.

The very babes in arms, with gesture droll,

Held out their little dimpled fists, and showed

The line that looked the straightest to the goal,

Whilst those who scarce could run, marked out the road.

Rest none required; but, ever and anon,

Fair hands brought food and drink, and sped them on.

CXIX.

As when a swarm of bees, with busy hum,

Quit the ancestral hive, and filmy wings,

Asudden stirred by instinct deep if dumb,

Sweep through the air in long continuous strings,

But when at length to their true bourne they come,

The loose lines close, and the dense phalanx clings

To mouth of hollow trunk, or pendent eaves,

Or drooping branch, feathered with summer leaves;

CXX.

So, by one common inspiration led,
The myriad hearts that each from honeyed home
At country's call unhesitating sped,
Winging their way down hills, through fields, o'er foam,
Now in sporadic files no more dispread,
Swarmed at the Sabine heights that look towards Rome,
There where Nomentum still keeps, half-consoled,
Its Latin name and Bacchic fame of old.

CXXI.

But what are these thinned ranks? Sure, all the flower
Of youth and prowess in the teeming land
Was hither blown, and in this crowning hour
Should crest the grassy peaks whereon we stand!
Have chilling winds or some perfidious shower
Wilted the growth, sun and soft breezes fanned?
Where are the myriad myriads we beheld,
Swelling the march, as streams by rills are swelled?

CXXII.

Ah! many a towering deed, winged by the heart,

And born to touch the very heaven of hope,

Is by the paltering brain denied its part,

And doomed its way by the vile earth to grope.

Aims that should speed, straight as the sharp-tipped dart,

And from their golden bourne nor swerve nor slope,

Fall short and all askew, if slackened string,

Or wavering hand, ruffle their well-fledged wing.

CXXIII.

E'en so, when, roused by patriotic peal,

The fair peninsula awoke, and straight

Poured her male legions to the tryst of steel,

The shivering dupes that still on Fortune wait,

Watching the tricksy harlot's flimsy wheel,

And dub their sycophancy craft of state,

Curbing brave mettle with base crook'd alarm,

Chilled her warm heart, and paralysed her arm.

E

CXXIV.

Ay, Rome or Death! A goodly cry. But mark

Which way the Gallic weathercock doth point.

It sets to fair! Then, gallant hearts, embark!

Stay! Look, it veers to foul! Great deeds, aroynt!

Be sheathed, ye swords! Encompass us, O dark,

And hide our hopes! The times are out of joint.

Swift to the frontier! fling the rash fools back!

What boot brute blades, when kingly brows are black?

CXXV.

'Twas but a purblind chanticleer that crowed;

The dawn is not yet here. Sleep on; 'tis night—

'Tis night, we say. Skulk each to his abode,

And snore till central suns proclaim the light.

The bright presumptuous star that erewhile showed

In mimicry of day, is quenchëd quite!

Abed once more, till the true orient gleams,

And lull your fluttering hopes with feeble dreams!

CXXVI.

And with these dominant commands there came
Confounding rumours, such as rend the soul
Of solid purpose; gusts that blow the flame
Of bright resolve now high now low, and roll
Round it a vaporous smoke, and thuswise tame
The limbs of those it lanterns to the goal;
Rumours begot by Hope on Fear, and nursed
By Spite, malignant hag that loves the worst.

CXXVII.

Where was the Chief? Had he yet left his isle?
Yes; foiling nimble lurchers of the law,
He treads the mainland. Did a sceptic smile?
Swift was the answer: here is one who saw . . .
Ay! but how now? A dungeon's well-clamped pile
Coffins his rashness. He will burst it . . . Faugh!
Back to Caprera, oath-bound, see him led,
To gnaw his heart out on its barren bed!

CXXVIII.

So of the hosts the glad alarum brought

From wide and far, with pulses all aglow

To rove the course they long had scoured in thought,

Some to the frontier, harebrained, rushed, and lo!

In nets unkingly cunning stretched, were caught.

Others more wary, after footsteps slow,

Turned and limped homewards, back to whence they drew,

Their paths no more refreshed by hope's sweet dew.

CXXIX.

But some there were whom nor recurrent fit

Of aguish doubt could from fixed beat divert,

Nor, wedded to the sword, divorce from it

Long tortuous wiles or sovereign summons curt.

What! Turn back now! No! though the earth should split,

And from its wounds hell's lethal lava spirt,

Though Italy's heart should crack in fetching breath,

The die is cast, that falls for Rome or Death !

CXXX.

And these, if few, yet steadfast, o'er the rim

Which severed still the freedman from the slave,

Had crept or burst, and in embattled trim,

Five thousand breasts, wooed glory or the grave.

Purged of the waifs that on the surface swim

Of noisy Venture's swift but shallow wave,

Shrunk was their volume now, calm, clear, and deep,

E'en as the cataract's, ere adown it leap.

CXXXI.

But on the mountainous ledge that dips towards Rome,

They still hung pausing; for the Chief yet lagged.

Cursed be the knaves that to his far-off home

Had yet again his limbs reluctant dragged!

Fools! would they coop the winds or curb the foam?

Soon flashed the news upon their spirits fagged,

That all unhelped he had slipped the net once more,

And wind and wave were wafting him to shore.

CXXXII.

Yes! steering tiny shallop, all alone,
From rock to rock 'mid perilous shoals, then tost
On tumbling billows by the mistral blown,
Till space 'twixt sea and sky seemed well-nigh lost,
Long ere the snarer guessed their bird was flown,
He gripped Sardinia's coast, its mountains crossed,
And thence by leal hands led and fair gales fanned,
Near Leghorn's beach leaped once again to land.

CXXXIII.

Never did group of orient devotees,
Whose triune God blends fire, and warmth, and light,
And who with straining eyeballs, prayerful knees,
And pulse impatient watch the sun first smite
The Persian hill-tops, hunger more than these
To see their sun-god, source of all their light,
Flame over the horizon, flood their veins
With heat and flame, and chase nocturnal pains.

CXXXIV.

Look, look! He cometh! a grey-crimson dawn,
A luminous apparition, scattering far
Chill mists of dim suspense, rollingly drawn
At sullen heel of Dark's retiring car.
Now peers broad Day, decked like a dappled fawn,
On whose fair forehead gleams a dewy star,
And which from covert brakes and darkling trees
Comes on apace, and freshly courts the breeze.

CXXXV.

Yes, yes, 'tis He! Now crisp your serried crests,
Ye bristling sons of Mavors' leonine loins!
Make one long frontage of your ample breasts,
And roar defiance to the world's four coigns!
Constrict your veins with ire! Swell out your chests
To breadth of battle, and your very groins
Invigorate with valour, that your tread
Nor halt nor falter till be Rome your bed!

CXXXVI.

Now swift to arms and flashing ranks they flew,
Shoulder to shoulder, heart by brave heart, ranged,
Quick with whose every beat He nearer drew.
Yes! 'tis the Chief, from venture unestranged,
As when his grasp the Bourbon Hydra slew
At tough Marsala, and a kingdom changed.
Upon his brow were threatening thunders piled,
But round his mouth Love's playful lightnings smiled.

CXXXVII.

Oh! now, no more from flinging round the neck
Of long-awaited sire white arms of joy,
Can chiding voice some doting daughter check,
Than did in these stern discipline destroy
Worship's strong instincts. They no longer reck
Arresting bonds ; they break their ranks, deploy
In wild disorder, press his form around,
And with mad shouts make the glad hills resound.

CXXXVIII.

"My children!" when the jubilant tumult waned,

With resonant clear voice he said, "I am here.

The French Jove's minions thought to hold me chained,

Lest I spread fire through this Cimmerian sphere.

Oh! how his eagle rent me as I strained

To rid me of my rock's engyving gear!

But herculean Destiny, which foils

Olympian counsels, came and cut my toils.

CXXXIX.

"And lo! I stand amidst you yet once more,

Sons of my heart and scions of my soul!

I see ye are still, all that ye were of yore,

The valorous stuff Alcmene's self might foal.

Behind, lies shame in ambush,—peril before.

Which do ye choose? Speak! whither is our goal?"

He paused; and like a thunderclap, the breath

Of their charged breasts bellowed, "To Rome or Death!"

CXL.

"'Tis well. Look there!" And as he spake they turned,

Following his finger with immediate eyes.

" There, there is the vent for which your lives have burned,

Your goal or grave, your sepulchre or prize.

Gods! where the suckling she-wolf's bosom spurned

The cruel priest's decision, darkly wise,

The foul hyæna's bastard litter tugs

At Italy's breast, poisoning our Mother's dugs!

CXLI.

" Will ye not, stalwart war-hounds, help me scare

The unclean foster-whelps from such a shrine ?—

This brood of Hell, that Heaven's fair front would wear,

From hearths which, even in ruin, keep divine;

Ruins, your own inheritance ? Now swear

By all the godhood in Rome's royal line,

By the Republic's virtue, by the brow

Of Empire calm, ye will reclaim them now!

CXLII.

"Lend me your youth, I give to you my years,

The steadfast wisdom of the life that hangs

Upon Death's gaze and calmly waits the shears,

Nor cares o'ermuch when the dark portal clangs.

So that I see the glimmer of your spears

Frighting the foemen's eyes, and mark your fangs

Fast in the hirelings fleeing from the list

Of final war, then let me be dismissed.

CXLIII.

"My task will then be finished. But I waste

In sterile words the sunlight. Now, to arms!

Yon citadel, within whose walls disgraced

A host of motley mercenaries swarms,

The savour of your valour first shall taste.

Now blow the sanguine bugle's shrill alarms!

Cleansed of its foul Batavian marsh-spawned boors,

Monte Rotondo must, ere dark, be yours!"

CXLIV.

Scarce had the warm words died upon his lips,

Than loud the clarion's circling summons rang.

But, as the lightning thunder-peal outstrips,

So, ere the notes were out, the martial gang

Glittered in arms, and as the staghound slips

The chiding leash, unto the foray sprang.

Youth in their hearts, Hope in their eyes there gleamed,

And Victory a beckoning goddess seemed.

CXLV.

Though light their panoply, their valour great.

No Vulcan's limping thunderbolts delayed

With cumbrous help their impetus elate ;

Theirs the straight barrel and the swooping blade,

The fleet advance—the pause—the crouching gait—

The forward rush—the well-seized ambuscade ;

Till in their trusty lines spread out, they feel

The circled city with a grasp of steel.

CXLVI.

Then straight its pulse responded. Loudly bayed
The deep-mouthed cannon from the walls, and woke
The slumbering citadel, which swiftly made
Its mouth a teeming womb whence martial folk,
Born ready-armed, swarmed to the rampart's aid,
Crested the walls, and glimmered through the smoke
Of sulphurous din, whose war-clouds thundered black
'Gainst the long sinuous hills, which bellowed back.

CXLVII.

Through such tough mail how find or force a way?
Like wave on wave of the untiring tide
Some granite cliff still shivers into spray,
Or like to sharp-toothed sleuth-hounds swept aside
And gored by antlered fugitive at bay,
So was their fury now by force defied,
Their rolling crests of valour beaten back,
And each fresh spring and grip a foiled attack.

CXLVIII.

No ponderous bolts of dead destruction hewed
A path to let their living fervour through,
'Gainst foes that winged, behind safe ramparts mewed,
Their shaftless barbs, invisible to view;
Whilst they with overt breasts and courage nude
Afresh their baffled onset must renew,
Making their lives a target, and their breath,
Aye spent, a bootless hecatomb to Death.

CXLIX.

Full many a dauntless form, nor scar nor scathe
From fell Melazzo's decimating fray,
Courting, that won, nor when life-streams did bathe
Volturno's river red, bore scratch away,
Ah! now sore swelled death's long and languid swathe,
And, all their bravery low, close-sickled lay;
Thin streams of blood dabbling their limbs forlorn,
As crimson poppies streak the down-cut corn.

CL.

Still catechumens, did Marsala's field
With sanguine chrism their soaring souls baptise ;
Calatifimi's blows their pledges sealed,
Their faith confirmed, their ardour rendered wise.
And now war's last anointment here annealed
Their stiffening limbs, and closed their filmy eyes;
And to where men nor fret nor slaughter, they
In agony of battle passed away.

CLI.

High as the waves, lashed by the winds of spring,
E'en so did roll the sanguinary tide,
From sultry noon till sunset, round the ring
Of still resisting ramparts, and the pride
Of strenuous hope, itself, recurrent, fling
Against the walls where, vain, it broke and died.
Then weary valour slackened, and the fray
In slow-retreating eddies ebbed away.

CLII.

"Fire me the gate!" the Chief exclaimed, "and smoke
These skulking vermin from their darksome holes!
Why waste your breath in many an idle stroke
Against the intangible air? Unearth the moles!
Look! you must break the shell to seize the yolk!
Then fire the gate, ye young and valorous souls!
Swiftly let torch and faggot be their guests,
And burn yourselves an entrance to their breasts!"

CLIII.

Then, under cover of the deepening dusk,
Whilst now the foe, in fancied fastness, drowned
With draughts of cheering wine the homely rusk,
Weening the day with conquering laurels crowned,—
With fascines girt and many a well-dried husk
Of last year's corn, soft to the gate they wound,
Whose solid jaws, deemed doubly safe till dawn,
Stood grimly clenched, with all the guards withdrawn.

CLIV.

Others too brought, but with like stealthy stride,

Bales of coarse tow in liquid resin steeped,

With kegs of shining pitch, and,—high and wide,

Faggot on straw, straw upon faggot heaped,—

Thrust them between, and then their torches plied.

Swift at the touch the prompt light crackling leaped,

And, darting tongues of fire from quivering frame,

The supine mass licked into maddening flame.

CLV.

Nor till the goodly pile was all ablaze,

Was the alarum raised within ; when straight

The deep carousers, smitten with amaze,

Snatching their arms, rushed madly to the gate.

But those into the darkness, far from gaze,

Softly drew off, and with hushed lips did wait,

To pour, with obvious aim that could not fail,

Through its reopening jaws a deadly hail.

F

CLVI.

And soon, the monstrous bars and bolts drawn back,
The huge gates groaned, then slowly opened wide,
And straight in front uprose the blazing stack,
Though through its gaps no foe could be descried.
So 'gan they all, emboldened, to attack
The burning barricade, and thrust aside
This fell approach of fire that strove to spread
To their defences its contagion dread.

CLVII.

Then as they rushed with ardour to undo
The invisible assailants' crafty task,
And with unguarded breasts swarmed full in view
Of those whom dark and distance still did mask,
Came sudden such a crashing volley through
The screen of sputtering twig and boiling cask,
That, staggering, back they fell, and, ambushed mesh
Dreading at hand, rolled back the gate afresh.

CLVIII.

But ere its ponderous lips could meet and clang,

The fiery mass fell in and choked its jaws.

Then once again a rattling volley rang

Straight through the chasm, and, all unseen the cause,

With deadly aim dealt many a mortal pang.

Then silence came,—a momentary pause,—

Then blinding smoke ; and then, all barriers snapped,

The gate, without, within, in flames was wrapped.

CLIX.

And all night long the well-fed bonfire rose,

Blackening the sky, lighting up all below,

From rolling plain, where surly Tiber flows,

To fixed Soracte's summit capped with snow.

On many a ruin Fate and fiercer foes

Had desolate left and void, a lurid glow,

Flickering, it flung, and flushed the long since sucked,

Dry, withered limbs of grey, gaunt aqueduct.

CLX.

The wolfish watch-dogs from uneasy sleep,

As though the moon were up, uprose and bayed,

While the rude herd, slow-roused from slumbers deep,

Crept from his hutch and the wild sight surveyed.

Leaning with hands that neither sow nor reap

On his long crook, all statue-like he stayed,

As one who wondered not, and in whose veins

The instinct flowed of fire and ravaged plains.

CLXI.

Unsheltered kine in unhelped labour lowed,

Coupling their throes with yet more deep dismay,

And stolid oxen, freed from yoke and goad,

Rolled their large eyes, and wondered was it day.

Troops of wild colts, no lord as yet bestrode,

Gathered in clouds, stopped, sniffed, then tore away ;

Whilst low-browed buffaloes, into terror lashed,

Through jungled swamp, snorting and bellowing, splashed.

CLXII.

It seemed as though the centuries had rolled
Their sepulchres back, and all the disarmed dead
Were coming forth anon, and, as of old,
Round Rome's seductive realm of ruin spread,
Would in their coils its feeble walls enfold,
And on its wreck a fresh destruction shed;
That Goth, Gaul, Vandal, Hun, would all conspire
To wrap what yet remained, in final fire!

CLXIII.

And still the greedy flames kept crawling round
Monte Rotondo's ivy-buttressed wall,
Whence gloomy owls, as if from under ground,
Flapped out, and with their melancholy call
Did ever and anon the deepening swound
Of dying ears with fantasies appal,
Vexing their souls with terror as they sank
Through yielding life into the deep dread blank.

CLXIV.

Nor till the dappled curtain of the East
Rose on the chorused dawn,—by surfeit choked,
Had the fierce fire from random foray ceased.
But long ere then, their sleepless limbs yet smoked
With grime of battle, and their rage increased
By yestreen's blood that still their garments soaked,
With bayonet couched and fury-flashing sword,
Through the charred portal had the Red-shirts poured.

CLXV.

Brief the resistance.　Like to waves that long
Thundering in vain 'gainst solid sea-wall's front,
When once a breach is battered, through it throng,
And nought withstands their onward-sweeping brunt ;
Or like to winds that, bursting barriers strong,
Drive drifted leaves along in wildering hunt,
So now before them, with resistless flow,
All craven shelter gone, they drave the foe.

CLXVI.

And still as they advanced, from thresholds freed
Came forth the exultant populace, and blessed
The arms that brought salvation to its need.
Their blackened hands the trembling grandsire pressed;
The tearful matron brought the welcome mead
Of mother's kiss; the soft-eyed maid caressed;
Whose brothers swelled their ranks, to lead them where
The routed hirelings clung to central lair.

CLXVII.

In a grim palace whose huge entrance seemed
Portcullis more than hospitable gate,
And through whose grim-barred embrasures there streamed
No ray of cheering sunshine soon or late,
Whose hoary walls were but too truly deemed
To boast the dungeon's thickness,—desperate,
And like to wolves whom baying throats surround,
The cowering foe had final covert found.

CLXVIII.

But when once more the threat of fire was hurled,
And torch and bavin to their hold were brought,
And round the basement tall the black smoke curled,
Quick from within a parley was besought,
And high o'erhead a small white flag unfurled.
Curt the conditions. These: All who had fought,
Would in the courtyard pile both gun and blade,
And straight across the frontier be conveyed.

CLXIX.

So on the morn of that auspicious day,
By valour wrenched, Monte Rotondo fell,
Making fagged limbs with freshening triumph gay,
And sinking hearts with surging hope re-swell
That henceforth neither foe nor fate could stay
Their supreme star and front invincible.
Lo! Yonder column rose, and tower, and dome,
In the blue air! Why not at once to Rome?

CLXX.

But calm-browed Wisdom's tranquillising smile
Checked their untimely ardour. " Not to-day.
Smeared with the sweat of victory, breathe awhile,
Nor tempt too much your yet half-mortal clay.
Another morn, and yon cross-crownëd pile,
That glistens in the sun, shall point your way ;
Nor shall its dome above the twilight soar,
A second time, ere Rome be God's once more ! "

CLXXI.

So wounds were blithely drest, and blood-stains dried,
And, as day broadened, deep siestas snatched ;
Some, stretched supine on the bare mountain-side,
Some, slumber-shaded under a pine detached.
And some lay gashed and shattered, open-eyed,
On pallets rough in hovels rudely-thatched ;
Whilst some, alack ! in their last bed were laid,
Nor heard o'erhead the beating of the spade.

CLXXII.

Far as the eye could scan,—and that, how far!—
No faintest mote flecked the crystalline air;
No fleecy cloudlet's zephyr-driven car
Sailed the blue dome, suspended everywhere;
The enthronëd Sun, Day's solitary star,
Steeped near and distant in a regal glare.
No breath, no stir, his godlike sway profaned,
But over all a shimmering silence reigned.

CLXXIII.

Lo! gaping temples with their gods all flown!
Lo! sacred founts whose waters well no more!
Niches, where statues long since overthrown
Leave concave void, mocking the might of yore!
Foundations scattered, soaring columns prone,
Wrecks of past tempests on a gaining shore,
From whose untrodden waste and stranded weeds,
The tide of Empire hour by hour recedes!

CLXXIV.

Here Nature weaved, from her invisible skein,
Unfading tapestry for roofless rooms ;
There, stripped by lust of Time, full many a fane
Bared to the gaze their desecrated wombs.
Arch upon arch, striding the long-drawn plain,
Mute guides that led, straight to the land of tombs,
Sudden stopped short, as though astonied grown,
Loth to advance, and bade you go alone !

CLXXV.

But at the base of circumambient hills,
Rome's waves of rolling blight break vain and die.
On Sabine slopes Plenty her horn refills,
And the ploughed earth laughs to the unploughed sky.
See, like a babe some gentle mother stills,
Its fretful Anio hushed, warm Tivoli lie,
It almost seems, crushed rather than caressed,
In a deep dimple of their sinuous breast.

CLXXVI.

Where burst the figs more honeyed or more fair,
Than where Frascati keeps the fame alive
Of philosophic Tusculum ; or where
Do patriarchal olives deeper dive
Than in the clods cleaved by the Alban share,
Grown in Ariccia's woods ? Where lustier thrive
The full-veined, breast-shaped pendants of the vine,
Than on Lavinia's Juno-blest incline ?

CLXXVII.

Nature withstands the shock of man's decay ;
No rust of time her glowing hue corrodes ;
A thousand sorrows leave her aspect gay ;
She smiles, forgetful, over wrecked abodes.
The popular breath, the despot's splendid sway,
Our shifting passions, oscillating modes,
Ephemeral creeds, changed gods, and altered goal,
Shake not the tenor of her firm-set soul.

CLXXVIII.

Deep in her heart the mighty secret lies
Which reconcileth hope and fear with Fate;
Yet she surrenders to our yearning eyes
Nought to instruct us, save her mien sedate.
In vain philosophy close questioning plies,
In vain her shrine doth science penetrate.
Dumb oracle she sits, and, like a star,
Shines but on those who look on her afar.

CLXXIX.

Now of heaven's azure sea the western bay
Began to heave with ripples of pure gold,
O'er which the bright-keeled argosy of day
Came proudly on, its venturous voyage told.
'Twixt plain and hill a deepening shadow lay;
The far-off summits changed from soft to bold;
All that the sun had traversed, to the eye
Shone clear, like life's past deeds, just ere we die.

CLXXX.

And, with the waning of the sultry glare,

About the camp a fitful movement grew.

Here, these prepared the evening meal, and there,

From bellied vats those beaded beakers drew.

Others with busy brows and muscles bare

Rubbed their accoutrements to flashing hue.

Some sang; and once, a solitary neigh

Shivered the air, then eddying died away.

CLXXXI.

Scarce a good bowshot from the bustling throng,

A farmstead stood, irregularly built,

Its walls of unhewn stone, yet square and strong,

Held in old days by arquebuse and hilt.

Alone of all the tenements along

Those scarce-clad heights by sunset softly gilt,

Nor strident voice nor desecrating hoof

Filled the apt shelter of its ample roof.

CLXXXII.

But if a curious eye had cared to scan
Its hidden life, two forms might now be seen,
Busy within; a godlike-statured man,
And grave-browed maiden, moulded like a queen:
A type to show what sovereign Nature can,
When stunting Progress cometh not between
Her and her handiwork; a shape unmarred
As, goddess-born, e'er fired the Scian bard.

CLXXXIII.

And like a queen of eld, her fingers fair
Played busily with stuffs of various dyes,
Red, white, and green, of which, with loving care,
She made, when shaped to strips of equal size,
A banner, such as Freedom's champions bear;
Whilst Gilbert watched her with unmoving eyes,
Propped 'gainst the threshold, and with absent hands
Smoothed a rough staff, mute slave of her commands.

CLXXXIV.

"'Tis done," she said, and as she said she rose.
"Now to the staff affix me Italy's flag,
And as the vane veers to the wind that blows,
So, once breeze-fluttered, never shall it lag
Behind the storm that breaks upon our foes,
Lead where it will, and though to death it drag!
Follow this symbol, Gilbert! you will find
Peril in front, but victory hard behind!"

CLXXXV.

The colours from her fair brave hands he took,
But quick the fair brave hands themselves he pressed,
Drawing them upwards, and with touch that shook,
Laid and soft held them 'gainst his ample chest.
And as some acorned oak bends low to look
On tender fern that girds its rugged breast,
So he, now bending her green form above,
Dropped in her lap the autumn of his love.

CLXXXVI.

"Yes, Miriam! to its flagstaff will I bind
Your banner fast, and follow it as true
As watching vane follows the wandering wind!
But when our blades have hewn a pathway through
To Rome or Death, then should I chance to find
The better doom, oh! unto me will you
Be as this beautiful pennon to its pole,
To bark its sail, unto the flesh its soul?

CLXXXVII.

"You, Miriam, you! my standard, symbol be,
And I could bear you through a cloud of foes!
The glorious colours you, upborne by me,
From battle's onset unto victory's close."
Then, holding flag and staff asunder, "See,
What soul or spell hath this apart from those?
But knit them close, and then, its flag unfurled,
E'en this shrunk branch might rouse a slumbering world!

G

CLXXXVIII.

"And yet a humbler, happier fate I crave,

Than to renew such task as brings us here.

Once let yon sky no longer roof a slave

In this fair land, and I our bark would steer

Back o'er that blue and syren-rippled wave,

To me through you, to you through instinct dear,

And, sweetly prisoned in your haunted isle,

Live in the sunshine of your wifely smile."

CLXXXIX.

She started at the words, and from his grasp,

Which kept them close, had all her form withdrawn,

But that he gripped her wrists with tightening clasp,

That left her helpless as some poor meshed fawn,

And with flushed breast did passionately gasp,

"Stay near me still, even as to night the dawn!

Fair life, fair love, with no dread gloom o'ercast,

Wherein I drown the darkness of my past!

CXC.

"Thy land, thy race, is mine, and thy young hopes
Are round my heart entwined, as a fair flower
Scales with its delicate bine and tendrilled ropes
The lonely gaps of some untenanted tower,
Where the bat burrows and the night-owl mopes.
O, be to me a beauty and a dower!
Fill me with light and colour, till men bless
Me, the poor wall, that props thy loveliness.

CXCI.

"Dead in the grave she lies, dead in the grave,
Who should have loved me, but she loved me not.
Pierced through the heart by passion's glittering glaive,
Thus did she leave me, who were best forgot.
Snowdrops and lilies her lone sepulchre pave,
White as the sheets over some infant's cot,
Where innocence lies sleeping. She too sleeps;—
Happier than one that wakes, and wants, and weeps.

CXCII.

" I would not wake her, for she was not mine.

Sound be her sleep and sweet; sweet be her dreams!

She will not dream of *me*. She was divine,

And I am earthly; so at least it seems.

Yet did she pour out all my life like wine,

And leave the goblet empty. O for streams,

Streams of full love that to the heart are wed,

As some deep river to its deeper bed!

CXCIII.

" That is not Love which is not loved : 'tis nought

But vacancy of pain, unfuelled fire,

A sigh by silence choked, a speechless thought,

Insanity of soul, diseased desire.

And Love is won no more than sold and bought;

'Tis a gratuitous giver, whom inspire

The Gods alone, whom we, alas! forsook.

The fault was mine. She gave me—what I took.

CXCIV.

" Perchance I speak a mystery; but with more
I must not violate thine ears.   Yet, oh!
If I should reach the heaven where my wings soar,
All that thou wouldst, then, Miriam, shalt thou know.
Into thy soul I all my soul will pour,
As into ocean swollen rivers flow,
Whose streams withal diminish not, but still,
As on they roll, fresh far-off waters fill.

CXCV.

" Streams roll not back, nor deem that I e'er could
To that dim past revert which was my bane.
I am as one who quits a darksome wood,
And sees before him sunlight-smiling plain,
Thankful to stand no more where late he stood.
Country and kin to me were symbols vain.
Thou art my kindred, and thy land shall be
Land of my love and true nativity.

CXCVI.

"But"—and yet tighter, as he spoke, he clenched

His nervous grasp—"by the Enduring Powers,

By all the tears that ever drowned and drenched

The cheeks of hopeless love through lonely hours,

Whose parching fires can by no tears be quenched,

By thy sire's ashes, by the sacred flowers

That roof thy mother's grave, I thee conjure,

Spare me not now! Strike home; I will endure.

CXCVII.

"Strike, but once only! I can nurse that pain;

Nurse it in solitude which doth repair

Even worse wounds than that. But there's a chain

No mortal twice consentingly would bear,—

The chain which binds with its tormenting strain

Two pulsing lives that one life do not share.

Love me with love that knows nor ebb nor flow,

As I love thee! or, Miriam, bid me go!"

CXCVIII.

Thereat he loosed her hands, and his own fell,

Mute, to his side ; and like some giant stone,

Poised on its base by old enchanter's spell,

So that it rocks e'en to a touch alone,

So now he stood, mightily movable,

And through the magic art fair Love doth own,

Spite his strong manhood, ready to be stirred

By the soft touch of her responsive word.

CXCIX.

A moment mute remained she, with her head

Bent on its stem, like some dark crimson rose

When winds have been too rough, which, since, have fled.

But soon, like bud that to the sunlight blows,

Her face she lifted to his gaze, and said,

" Did he not tell thee ? For indeed he knows.

He wrung my secret from me on the day

Our joyous war-bark bounded o'er the bay."

CC.

"What!" he exclaimed, as future, present, past,
Before his eyes in one black cloud did swim ;
"What! Godfrid! Comes he then once more to blast
My hopes of heaven? Oh! how Love's sight is dim!"
"O, thou mistak'st me quite!" she cried, aghast;
"For thee he pleaded, and I answered him,
Straight from my soul, as now I answer thee :—
Love me, and I will listen,—when Rome is free !

CCI.

"Till then,—but hark!" And ere one grateful word
Could from his bosom burst to ease his joy,
Out through the threshold, like a startled bird,
She flew, he following like an eager boy.
And lo! the camp with some strange news was stirred,
And, as a flock of wild-fowl to decoy,
Skimming the reedy pool, are blindly urged
On instant wing, towards one point converged.

CCII.

Thither, too, Miriam, Gilbert to her side
Still keeping close, all breathless made her way,
The rush of supple striplings opening wide
To let them pass athwart the armed array.
"'Tis the brave band returned from Rome," one cried.
"Then Godfrid's back!" both in one breath did say;
While she, with voice low as a breathing shell,
Murmured, scarce heard, "Pray Heaven! alive and well!"

CCIII.

Soon were all doubts dispelled; for towards the crest
Of the steep range whose face towards Rome is set,
A handful stood, by thirsty march distressed,
Hot, haggard, silent, dashed with gore and sweat;
And in their midst, towering o'er all the rest,
As 'mong tall fir-trees tall pine tops them yet,
Stood Godfrid, gloomy, dark with dust and smoke,
And to the gathering crowd thus curtly spoke:—

CCIV.

"Yes, we are back, or those at least you see,

A remnant, safe ; the best are left behind:

Of freedom reft that others might be free,

Or dead, that worse than dead fresh life might find.

Cairoli fell o'erborne, one against three,

But not till two of three first fed the wind.

His Spartan dam may smile; one son remains;

Not here,—but wounded, captive, and in chains.

CCV.

"What did I hear you ask? Does Rome not rise?

Who rises with the heel upon his neck,

Or greets the dawn with joyfulness, whose eyes,

Long shorn of sight, the greedy vultures peck?

Alas! Of heaven-fed Freedom's lusty cries,

What can poor deaf priest-suckled serflings reck?

Rome rise? Yes—when you raise her. Not till then.

Shall she long wait you? Not if ye are men!"

CCVI.

With which, the keen-eared group aside he ploughed,

And, greeting Miriam with fraternal speech,

Passed, linked with her and Gilbert, from the crowd

To that lone dwelling placed beyond the reach

Of the camp's tumult. Then, like storm-charged cloud,

The black news circled round, each questioning each,

And vowing deep, as swift the story spread,

To rouse the living and avenge the dead.

CCVII.

So Dark fell gloomily upon the camp,

Stifling the voice of day; save where anon

The faithful sentinel's recurrent tramp

Fretted the silent air. No fair moon shone,

Nor mute attendant stars. The night-dews damp

Drenched sleep-laid locks which no soft shrouds did don;

Thankful in turf-smoothed mound and stone to press

A witching pillow for their weariness.

CCVIII.

They sleep; they dream; they will awake. But oh!
How many folded now 'neath slumber's wing,
Whose stream of life doth darkly-silent flow,
Filtered through dreams to bright awakening,
Will e'er again this sweetening lethe know,
This subterranean plunge whence newly spring
Health's sparkling currents, every thirst to slake?
Ah! they will sleep once more, but not to wake!

CCIX.

Deep, dark, unending slumber will be theirs,
Whereto there comes no dawn nor pipe of birds,
No smell of green buds bursting unawares,
Nor milk-sweet breath of dewy-ankled herds.
For them mute Death the ebon couch prepares;
For them the Fates chant low the fatal words.
They will awake, to die! Why cannot Sleep
Locked in its arms their souls for ever keep?

CCX.

Lo! they awake, they rise, and spring as light
From their rough beds as hare from grassy seat;
Hailing the spears of Dawn, whilst routed Night
Flings out a mist to cover her retreat.
But all in vain her subterfuge of flight,
Pursuer than pursued is yet more fleet;
And, all her shivering banners seized and furled,
Day reigns, unchallenged, o'er a glittering world!

CCXI.

Then quick the martial heights and slopes began
To prick and burgeon into armèd life;
The dense red ranks spread out like gaudy fan,
To deep-toned drum and treble-fluted fife.
From mouth to mouth the gladsome rumour ran,
The hour was here to kiss the lips of strife,
With battle's breast to blend embrace and breath,
And leap, delirious, into Rome or Death!

CCXII.

And straight towards Rome their frowning crests were set,
Just as storm-freighted thundercloud doth first
Roll wide its waves of universal threat,
Then blackens towards the point where it will burst;
Whilst, like a land the fickle rains forget,
All parched and fissured with still deepening thirst,
Rome arid lay, longing to hear the brawl
Break overhead, and feel the black drops fall.

CCXIII.

But as they gazed, and every bosom rose,
High-leavened with the thought of combat nigh,
Far off they saw, as when a ground-mist grows,
Or distant copse shows feathery to the eye
When first the early-budding sallow blows,
About the walls a haze ambiguous lie,
Which, when it once had shape and substance ta'en,
Rolled itself out, and crept along the plain.

CCXIV.

Shortly the moving mist began to gleam
And glitter, as when tips of orient rays
Glint on the ripples of a rolling stream,
Until it glowed one scintillating blaze,
Flickering and flashing in each morning beam.
And then they knew it was no vaporous haze,
But foe come forth,—bayonet, and blade, and gun,—
Shining and shimmering in the dancing sun.

CCXV.

Swift through their lines a thrill electric ran,
And, as it died, girt by that faithful few
Whose spendthrift lives had still been in the van
Since first his banner of redemption flew,
'Midst men heroic looking more than man,
Serenely strong, the Chief came full in view;
While through the ranks, with sabre-sounding clang,
A shout of welcome and defiance rang.

CCXVI.

"Hail, noble champions of a noble Cause!"
Flashing them back their greeting, thus he spake.
"See, Fortune smiles. The beast whose greedy claws
Ye have come to clip, doth from his covert break,
And, spurred by desperate terror, hither draws.
Now in your hands your shafts avenging take,
And bide his onset! We will wait him here,
And let the rash fool rush upon the spear.

CCXVII.

"Then shall his lair be yours. Gods! what a lair!
The very cradle of your name and race;
To Roman loins where Sabine women bare
A lusty birth from violent embrace:
Sons sternly strong, daughters divinely fair,
Celestial those in force as these in face,
Who, not unmindful of their getting, curled
Their sinewy arms around a ravished world!

CCXVIII.

"What! do ye vaunt their blood still warms your veins?
Are ye the lineage of that splendid rape?
Then, of the world they won ye, what remains,
From Parthia's plains to Calpe's final Cape?
O'er your sires' empire who is he that reigns?
Where is their sceptre, if ye boast their shape?
What, of the wide inheritance their zone
Of conquest girdled, do ye call your own?

CCXIX.

"Look! where your sires, disarmed by Love's decree,
To their all-willing brides at length were wed,
The Gallic harlot, fetched across the sea,
With venal limbs fouls your ancestral bed!
Your home, your hearth, your very nursery,
Where Roman babes on Roman tales were fed,
Hath grown a den defiled, a place of shame,
Barbarians mock, and patriots blush to name!

H

CCXX.

"Where trod the Jove-crowned conquerors of earth,
The stealthy shaveling slipshod creeps along;
Where rang the echoes of triumphant mirth,
The trembling monk mumbles his drowsy song.
On the twin hill where Empire took its birth,
And all the victor eagles used to throng,
A spurious Cæsar pours his legions foul,
And flings his ægis o'er each crouching cowl!

CCXXI.

"And do ye live and breathe? Now live no more,
Save ye can purge the palace and the fane
Of prince and priest who barter grace 'gainst gore,
And God's and Cæsar's name alike profane.
Is Italy so fair, their native shore
Bounds their barbarian appetite in vain?
Vainly the Alps arise, vain rolls the wave?
Then sate their greed of soil.—Give them a grave!"

CCXXII.

Then with brief words, and indicating hand,
Along the heights and broken slopes he spread
The little cohorts of his clustered band.
Some in the shrunken streamlet's stony bed
He showed to crouch, and others bade to stand
Behind the waving ridge's sheltering head,
And watch, with eye alert and firelock low,
To deal dark death on the presumptuous foe.

CCXXIII.

For those, in loose sporadic order ranged,
Cover he found in vineyards densely green,
As with the wand of conjuring Mars he changed
To panoply of war their peaceful screen,
From all sweet pristine purposes estranged.
Terraced and sloped to form the fruitful scene
Of happy toil, behold them frowning fort,
And cruel jungle for man's tigerish sport!

CCXXIV.

And where the grey-trunked olive's purpling beads
Glistened among its shifting-coloured sprays,
He dotted children of the mountain-meads,
Who mark the chamois with unerring gaze
On track that only to the snow-line leads;
Whilst others in the down-cut corn and maize,
Cut but unstacked, he bade in ambush wait,
Patient as vengeance, pitiless as fate!

CCXXV.

Ah! thus this fair and frolic world, whose lap
Teems and runs o'er with oil, and corn, and wine,
Whose veins, for ever young, the generous sap
Of Plenty, stored in life's mysterious mine,
Still mounts, can human madness and mishap
Drench with salt tears more barren than the brine;
Where love and song should wreathe their brow with flowers,
Thus rage and anguish fill the hateful hours.

CCXXVI.

Hark! the sharp challenge of a rifle rings
Shrill through the air! then all again is still;
Save where its eddying echo faintly clings
To the deep hollows of some distant hill.
But soon the breeze a fuller message brings,
Another,—and another yet,—until
A fitful musket-rattle spreads around,
And silence seems but waiting upon sound.

CCXXVII.

Awhile from hill and slope no answer came;
Though many a sharp-fanged messenger of death
Tore through the leafy vine-stem's tender frame,
Scorched the grey trunks with its malignant breath,
And set the shocks of ripened maize aflame.
But as when long a storm-cloud lingereth,
And, since it loometh black, men wonder why
Its earth-aimed javelins linger in the sky,

CCXXVIII.

But when at length it bursteth overhead,

It bursteth all at once, and serried hail

Flashes and rattles on the torrent's bed,

And lays the corn, flat as the thresher's flail ;

So now, at lagging signal swiftly spread,

The scowling muzzles pointing towards the vale

Hurled on the foe a hurricane of steel,

That made the foremost fall, the hindmost reel.

CCXXIX.

But brief the check.   As when a fleecy wreath,

The pale outrider of the mist that wraps

The vale below, up 'gainst the craggy teeth

Of some tall peak where never pinion flaps,

All vainly curls and melts, but from beneath

Fresh waves of white roll up, till cloudland laps

Steep, height, and summit, and the cliffs that scale

The spheres of snow, in ever-densening veil ;

CCXXX.

So, though the cloud of skirmishers that erst,

In tenuous haze, up from the valley crept,

Insidious,—slow,—'gainst that firm frontage burst,

And into vaporous nothingness was swept,

Still rank on rank, each denser than the first,

Rolled on, and every point it gained it kept,

Till slope and range, held by the red-shirt folk,

Were wrapped in wreaths of dusky-volumed smoke.

CCXXXI.

But for a while, though the conspiring fumes

Of earth and heaven his lofty brow enshroud,

The mountain monarch, crowned with snowy plumes,

Shakes off the mist, majestically proud,

And all his clear serenity resumes.

And, none the less, from that tormenting cloud

Did the long range of valour on the height

Emerge once more, and glitter in the light.

CCXXXII.

Not all the spendthrift missiles of attack
Had from resistance torn one rood away,
Though trampling Death had roughly scored his track
With many a maiden's joy and mother's stay.
Some gazed at heaven with sightless orbs, alack!
Some, as asleep, among the vine-leaves lay;
And some were prone, with faces to the earth,
Hiding from sight their darkness and their dearth.

CCXXXIII.

Now must be craven bolts, winged from afar,
Exchanged for bristling weapons, face to face,
And all the distant dalliance of war
Discarded for the grip of close embrace.
"Now, Latin lads, show of what strain ye are,
And prove the unslacked mettle of your race
Against these mongrels of a lineage lewd,
The bastard sons of sires your sires subdued!"

CCXXXIV.

So through the hush of momentary truce
Rang the Chief's clarion voice. But from his lips
Scarce had the words been fledged, than, as a sluice
Opens and all its pent-up water slips,
Was all the volume of assault let loose,
And, wave on wave, the flashing bayonet-tips
Came streaming on, an ever-broadening ring,
Crested with banners of the Pontiff-King.

CCXXXV.

Wave upon wave: As, when on some long shore
The tide comes rolling in, in ridgy sheets,
Surge after surge, with hollow-bosomed roar,
Plunges and breaks, then hurriedly retreats,
And the stunned strand stands solid as before,
But swift a fresh on-coming billow meets
The flying foam, and carries it along,
Back to the assault, with volume doubly strong;

CCXXXVI.

So, endless, rolled the ridges of attack,

Line after line, valour at valour's heel;

Surged, roared, rushed, broke, then fell in fragments back,

Shattered and shivered 'gainst that shore of steel.

Yet waxed not then the tide of onset slack,

But as each ruined rank was seen to reel,

Another,—longer,—stronger,—onwards dashed,

And o'er the flying eddies curled and crashed.

CCXXXVII.

Thus, for as long as draws the mistress moon

The waters of the deep one way, the tide

Of fury that had first set in at noon

Flowed onwards, till, though full, 'twas still defied,

Nor for a while or gained or ebbed. But soon

The sea of utmost ardour 'gan subside;

The living waves waxed fainter and more few,

And from the beach, discomfited, withdrew.

CCXXXVIII.

Then forth from copse and vineyard, orchard, grove,

Farmstead and stony torrent's shielding bank,

And deep-set pools where the tall cane-stems wove

For ambushed feet a cover dense and dank,

Rushing and trampling came a mighty drove,

That swiftly formed in many a hornèd rank,

And swarming on each open crest and crown,

Paused for the word, should launch their limbs adown.

CCXXXIX.

Full on the right of the embattled host,

Glimmered the generous blades that, flasht betimes,

First hewed a path to freedom :—Savoy's boast,

That hardy race, strung by subalpine rimes ;

With sea-bronzed breasts from curved Liguria's coast,

Lithe Lombard striplings tall as unpolled limes,

And high-browed sons of Venice, come to spread

The spell which, yestreen, raised her from the dead.

CCXL.

In close array, upon the left, was packed
The South's volcanic valour; Ætna's stock,
Ready to roll, a fiery cataract,
Down the hillside; Vesuvius' dark-eyed flock,
That in the blackness of the night had hacked
From their own limbs the fetter's cankerous lock;
And grave-faced exiles from great Rome itself,
Who long had scorned to share submission's pelf.

CCXLI.

And in the centre of the bright array,
The kernel of its courage, clustered those
Who sleepless watched the lifting lids of day,
And leaped to arms as Freedom's orient rose:
The gashed survivors of Marsala's fray,
Who fed Volturno's vultures with their foes;
And those who sware Marsala's well-kept vow,
A thousand falchions then,—a handful now.

CCXLII.

Here, mute as moulded marble, Godfrid stood,

With heart as quiet, and with hands as still,

As when the beaters flush some well-stocked wood,

Or drive wild wings upon the heathered hill.

Nigh him stood Gilbert, like in hardihood,

But who, with pulses bubbling like a rill,

Close as a shadow kept by Miriam's side,

And tightly grasped a banner triple-dyed.

CCXLIII.

As when ye saw her first among the vines,

Singing a hymn to Freedom, see her now,

Her dark eyes shining as the night-star shines,

And, bare, her black hair rippling from her brow!

Her crimson kirtle fell in martial lines

To her firm feet; and as round some full prow

The foam-pleats white alternate rise and rest,

'Neath snowy folds heaved her heroic breast.

CCXLIV.

But where to boddice and to kirtle bright
Were twined and loopèd vine-leaves erst attached,
Now, lashed across the kerchief's spotless white,
A silk green scarf the sister colours matched.
And when the trumpet shrilled for final fight,
From Gilbert's hand the banner quick she snatched,
Flung to the breeze its folds, and as the clang
Of battle-charge began, sonorous sang.

I.

Now by the might of Mavors' line!
   Now by the Brothers Twin!
Now by Lucretia's stroke divine,
   That quenched the Tarquin's sin!
By the decisive sword of old,
   Flung by the haughty Gaul,
When greedy Brennus clutched the gold,
   And, weighing, lost it all!

Now by great Scipio's blade that bit

  The Afric's breastplate through,

And by Rienzi's torch which lit

  Rome's vestal fires anew !

Awake ! Arise ! Lift up your eyes !

  And swear, from Alp to sea,

From the bending shore to the crags that soar,

  Our Italy, fair Italy,

Shall be one, shall be one and free !

2.

Ho ! Lombard banners, to the fore !

  Ho ! Savoy, clinch the rear !

Ho ! Volscian lads that hunt the boar

  With never-snapping spear !

Make of your thews a mighty wall,

  Like Antium made of yore,

That vain should smite the Libyan squall

  Her Fortune-favoured shore !

Ho! mountain breasts that beard the snows !
   Ho! arms that reave the main!
Ho! Tuscan hands that pluck the rose,
   And reap the yellow grain!
Awake! Arise! Lift up your eyes!
   And swear, from Alp to sea,
From the bending shore to the crags that soar,
   Brave Italy, proud Italy,
Shall be one, shall be one and free!

CCXLV.

More sang she not, for the soft-closing notes
In the tumultuous air scarce space had found ;
And e'en the chorus, hymned by thousand throats,
Was in the roar of thunderous onset drowned.
No more than voice of agony that floats,
When tempests swoop and winds and seas resound,
From slowly-sinking lips all loth to die,—
Soared their refrain, a muffled, feeble cry.

CCXLVI.

Not fiercer, blacker, sweeps the Alpine storm,

When gorges howl and the fir-forests crash ;

Not louder, ocean, when the dun waves form

Their monstrous heads, and rocks and breakers clash ;

Not straighter doth the avalanche enorm

Its jagged path through the dense pine-masts gash,

Than swept the impulse of their gathered will,—

At once wind, wave, and lauwine,—down the hill.

CCXLVII.

And like to serried trunks whose hoary tops

Toss, bend, and swing in the distracted air,

When some invisible hand the hollow stops

Of heaven's loud organ opens unaware

And rolls wind-music over wood and copse,

The bristling lines, soon as they heard the blare

And felt the brunt of that tempestuous shock,

Strenuous as sudden, 'gan to roll and rock.

I

CCXLVIII.

And as they rocked, yet fuller waxed the stress
Of that on-sweeping hurricane, that bore,
Strong against strength, 'gainst pity pitiless,
Where fierce the stand, fiercer in onset more,
And 'gainst resistance all resistlessness;
Till,—rank behind confused with rank before,
Column with square confounded, van with rear,—
Through the cooped host, fluttered the wings of Fear.

CCXLIX.

Then as wild coveys, when warm days have gone,
That equinoctial winds have swelled and packed,
Down the dun moor, a cloud of wings, come on,
And, as they flit, upon the heathery tract
And bracken-patches cast a shadow wan,
But when from screening wall have loudly cracked
The sportsmen's barrels, swift the wings divide
And over knoll and scaur fly far and wide;

CCL.

So the dense ranks that fenced the Triple Crown,

And, all unmindful of rebuke divine,

Drew Peter's sword afresh, soon as the frown

Of grim assault drew near in line on line

Of smoke and steel, flung blade and rifle down,

And scattering wide o'er dip and steep incline,

Their faces set where safety led the way,

And fled in wildered flakes of loose dismay.

CCLI.

Then all seemed won.   And as, when melting snows

Swell the famed stream that laves the Emilian plain,

Cooped 'twixt its banks awhile the river flows,

Rolling and raging towards the Hadrian main;

But once the lofty dykes that should enclose

Its rampant force, no more resist the strain,

Crumble and crack, then wide the waters spread

Round hamlet, farm, tall spire, and lowly shed:

CCLII.

So now the Red-shirt torrent, that at first
Steadied by curbing discipline had rolled,
Soon as it felt resistance' barriers burst,
Asunder swept and spread out uncontrolled ;
Dispersing as the fugitives dispersed,
By the wild rout made hazardously bold,
Till all along the line,—left, centre, right,—
Pursuit had waxed disorderly as flight.

CCLIII.

Yet not one fleeing face was turned to smite
The victor's rashness ; but away, away,
Like to scared cushat chased by ravening kite,
Sped each fleet foot,—fast—faster,—from the fray.
Then rang once more that war-cry of delight,
" Death ! Death or Rome !" through all the glad array
Of following triumph, whilst the cross-crowned dome,
Glistening afar, seemed to reëcho, " Rome !"

CCLIV.

When lo! though nought as yet could they descry
Save friends behind and scudding foes before,
Afresh the bolts of death began to fly,
Burst forth afresh the bellowing cannon's roar.
So thick the steely hail, they scanned the sky
To see if Heaven itself perchance did pour
The hissing missiles down, and foully mar
With unfair stroke the hard-got spoils of war.

CCLV.

But even while they halted, and with eyes
Of wonder, not of terror, gazed around,
They saw the flying rout melt phantomwise,
And sudden, in its stead, as from the ground,
A new and wide-embattled host arise,
Waving bright banners with the eagle crowned;
Bristling in arms, gun, bayonet, sabre, lance,—
The glittering legions of imperious France.

CCLVI.

Then rage seized every breast; and once again,

By warlike instinct ordered, swift they shrank,

Like scattered flock the tall-crooked shepherds pen,

Into close file and steady marshalled rank;

Though faster, thicker, rained upon them then

The lethal hail, and many a high heart sank,

To rise no more, on whom, a moment gone,

The lustrous sun of dawning victory shone.

CCLVII.

No more their jaded breath and sinews spurred

By triumph's bounding pulse, but every limb

Fainting beneath the weight of hope deferred,

Yet even then their ardour waxed not dim;

But as a beacon-fire, a moment blurred

By gusty rain and veiled in smoke-clouds grim,

Flares up anew, the fiercer for being quelled,

So higher, hotter, now their courage swelled.

CCLVIII.

Fagged against fresh, a handful 'gainst a host,

With nought but naked steel now left to cope

With every bolt that Mars and Vulcan boast,

'Gainst firm-set Fate a feebly desperate hope,

A half-spent tide against an iron coast,

See them once more, now as the sun-rays slope

Athwart their decimated ranks, advance,

And face the unbroken front of towering France.

CCLIX.

What patter of April shower on branch and bud

Is to grim winter's slantly-slashing hail,

What to the snow-swelled torrent's bounding flood

The trickling summer streamlet's loitering tale,

What woodland barrel to the cannon's thud,

What soft south zephyr to antarctic gale,

Such the steel shower that late their ranks did plough,

Was to the rifles' rain that rent them now.

CCLX.

'Twas as though thousand furnaces of death,

Fledging hot shafts in sulphur-teeming womb,

With inexhaustible volcanic breath

Winged them, unerring messengers of doom!

In vain, as swift as one form tottereth,

Another fills the void ; for him the tomb

Opens, and sucks him down. One more yet wades

These waves of death, then into darkness fades.

CCLXI.

In vain or force or feint, courage or skill,

Against a foe that seemed to multiply,

By some miraculous arm, its strength at will,

And, scattering death, never itself to die.

Maddened by pain, no more they cared to fill

Their widening gaps, but with a desperate cry,

Rushed in disordered valour, singly brave,

If not to make, at least to find a grave.

CCLXII.

And many found, yet not one eager edge

Of all that rushing steel e'er reached the foe ;

But, swept aside, as the wind sweeps the sedge,

Or, when the equinoctial furies blow,

Strong gulls are beaten back from beetling ledge,

And seek the shelter of the cliff below,

Those whom a foiling fate forbade to bite

The welcome dust, were swept away in flight.

CCLXIII.

Ah ! then those fled who never fled before,

And they who would have limb from limb been torn

Sooner than fly, by those, alas ! who wore

Their own proud badge, were backwards pressed and borne ;

Still with their faces to the cannon's roar,

Still with their nostrils breathing martial scorn,

But all as idly as defiant sail

Would beard the storm and ride against the gale.

CCLXIV.

And ever as in scattered rout they fled,

Back o'er the ground they late as victors trod,

The swift-pursuing steel hissed overhead,

While many a lip kissed the ensanguined sod.

And ah! full many a dying prayer was said,

As took the soul its farewell of the clod,

And deaf though Heaven seemed grown to cries and plaints,

Wild vows were breathed to long-forgotten saints.

CCLXV.

Once only did they turn and stand at bay.

'Twas when with eyes of fury they beheld

The pack of Gallic bloodhounds, fresh for fray,

Joined in pursuit, and its fierce music swelled,

By the base mongrels who had slunk away

Scared by their presence, but now yelped and yelled

Louder than all, and strove with fangs unfed

To tear the backs before whose breasts they fled.

CCLXVI.

Then every brow that not in sleep was laid,

And every foot that still could crawl to front,

And every hand that yet could wield a blade,

Wheeled round to stem that sanguinary hunt.

No mouthing cannon lent its strenuous aid;

Nought had they now but steel whose edge was blunt

With hours of slaughtering, nought but naked arms,

And that fine rage which, even in failure, charms.

CCLXVII.

And quickly with their swords they hewed a place

Around a rude low wain, at daybreak filled

With ammunition long since blown to space,

Yoked with two steers; one in war's shambles killed,

The other still with sleek obedient face

Standing, as though in peaceful furrow stilled

By master gone to take his simple meal,

When the tall church-tower bells at mid-day peal.

CCLXVIII.

And black with battle-smoke and splashed with gore,

By one wheel towered Godfrid, and by one,

Gilbert: each faithful to the vow he swore,

That Rome or Death should crown the setting sun.

And like to her, Bellona hight of yore,

Into the wain, carrying the flag she spun,

Lightly leaped Miriam, all its folds unflung,

And o'er the din these sounding curses sung :—

I.

May thy banners be rolled in the mire,

Thine eagles be trampled in dust!

Thy villages blackened by fire,

Thy daughters devoted to lust!

May thine armies be smitten with pallor,

Thy strong places treat with the foe;

May a by-word be made of thy valour,

Thy glory be blotted like snow!

May the spur of the insolent stranger

    Be clanked o'er thy thresholds at night ;

May he make of thy cradles a manger !

    May he take in thy beds his delight !

May he drink of thy vintages fairest,

    May he feast on thy harvest of years ;

Mayst thou hear, in the hour thou despairest,

    His laugh and the clash of his spears !

Mayst thou grovel for mercy, nor find it,

    Mayst thou bend 'neath his burden thy back !

Mayst thou taste of the lash, and behind it

    The scorn of the tyrants that crack !

May none of thy children exhibit

    One virtue, redeeming thy name ;

Mayst thou buy off the victor with tribute,

And Time and Eternity gibbet

    Thy downfall with shame !

2.

And when once the best seed of thy loins

    Thou hast bartered for pardon and case,

And the conqueror, clinking thy coins,

    Turns his back as thou crawl'st from thy knees,

May the children his pity shall leave thee,

    The swords they late laid at his feet,

Snatch, and, cowardly parricides, cleave thee,

    And fling thee to jackals to eat!

May brother take courage 'gainst brother,

    The son not be scared by the sire,

May the child vent his wrath on the mother,

    Thy heroes on women their ire!

May on thee all the fiends that e'er jabbered

    Their discord in hell wreak their powers,

And that steel find in priests' flesh a scabbard,

    For a Priest, thou now plungest in ours!

In the ways of thy beautiful city,

    May Slaughter as traffic be thick,

May Revenge wade through blood without pity,

   Till slayer with slaying grow sick!

And when Carnage is gorged, oh! then after,

   To the demons of fire be thou sworn,

That shall rage around rooftree and rafter,

And leave thee, the loathing and laughter

   Of ages unborn!

CCLXIX.

But long before the execrating strain

Thus clashed to close, the many-dinted blades

Had carved a goodly circle round the wain,

And a new batch of miscreants to the Shades,

Howling, had sent, whose recreant fellows fain

In flight found safety, like to venturous maids

That follow the retreating sea, but swift

Fly, when the waves afresh their foam-crests lift.

CCLXX.

And all alone, her banner in her hand,

And all the Furies towering in her eyes,

Upon the wain, electrically grand,

Like unto one sole cloud in thunderous skies

The lurid sunlight smites, did Miriam stand,

Marking the battle-surges fall and rise,

And, 'mid the clash of swords confusedly grouped,

Where Gilbert's flashed, and Godfrid's, poising, swooped.

CCLXXI.

But soon the doughty arms that thus had gained

From struggle new new strength, were left to waste

Their strokes in air, since for each foot they gained

By prowess, fear their foes a rood displaced.

Then thick the strange miraculous missiles, rained

From weapons such as flesh had never faced

Since war was born of discord, 'gan once more

On bravest front death and dismay to pour.

CCLXXII.

Then many fled, and those who fled not fell;

And, from that moment, Miriam 'mong the erect

Nor Gilbert saw nor Godfrid. 'Mid the swell

And surf of carnage lay their valour wrecked.

And ere she could descend and rush to well

Her love in dying ears,—unruled, unchecked,

The tide of flight came on, and as the spray

Lifts the light seaweed, swept her steps away.

CCLXXIII.

The last she saw was that mute patient steer

Join its yoke-fellow in death's darkened stall,

Where it may slumber peaceful all the year,

Dreading no bondsman's stroke, no master's call.

The rest was like the tumult in the ear

Of waters o'er the drowning, or the pall

That falls on fainting eyes when pulses reel,

And even the living brain forgets to feel

CCLXXIV.

Down dropped the sun as though ashamed to stay,

And, as he veiled his eyes, above—around,—

The sky all blushed the colour of the fray,

Reflecting deep the crimson of the ground.

Then slowly, sadly, died the flush away

On Nature's cheek, in horrent pallor drowned;

Till even pallor's self no more could bloom,

And o'er her face there crept a hueless gloom.

CCLXXV.

But still through gloaming and the deepening dusk,

Incessant skimmed the frantic feet of flight,

As flies the fawn before the wild-boar's tusk

When hunger sends him raging through the night.

And if they stopped to grope for remnant rusk

Left in their wallets who no more should bite

The sweet fresh bread of home, or stooped to cool

The fire of burning throats in brackish pool;

CCLXXVI.

Anon the dark-aimed javelins of death
Robbed the poor life they fain had sought to ease,
Or spurred afresh their still sore-panting breath.
And as one hears a ghost on every breeze,
When between midnight tombs one hasteneth,
So did their fearful fancy picture trees,
Ruin, and rock, another,—final,—host,
To speed their steps to Pluto's gloomy coast.

CCLXXVII.

Into sparse wattled sheep-pens many crept,
And by the rude but pitying herd were hid
Among his flock that, all inhuman, slept.
But their bed-fellows closed not weary lid,
And when pursuit's fierce waves had past them swept,
Up from the strange, warm, throbbing couch they slid,
And to their host, beneath the starlight pale,
'Mid sobs of rage they stammered out their tale.

CCLXXVIII.

They told him how the dawn was rocked with hope,
How noon had seen the hirelings' onset foiled,
How they, triumphant, bounded down the slope,
And then,—with lips that faltered, blood that boiled,—
How their spent strength had with new foes to cope,
And Italy's dream, touching its goal, was spoiled!
Then, speech engulfed in surges of the breast,
Aghast they stood, and, silent, looked the rest!

CCLXXIX.

Till one just mustered stertorous breath to tell
The shepherd son of Romulus who those were
That with their hellish sorcery broke the spell.
Whereat the hind shook all his matted hair,
And to their curses joined his curses fell;
Brandished his crook, and struck it through the air
Against the ground, as though it were a spear,
And called the avenging gods below to hear!

CCLXXX.

But long ere timid stars stole forth to peer

Through latticed heaven on what the day had done,

Monte Rotondo saw gaunt forms of fear

Pour in, and through her streets unhalting run.

A haggard troop, pale, footsore, nerveless, sere,

Oh! how unlike those heralds of the sun,

Who, ripe for victory, with feet elate

Had carried fire and freedom through her gate!

CCLXXXI.

Into Mentana's squalid ways,—for there

A little band, at daybreak left behind,

Still kept unbroken front,—the wounded bare

The dying, fain some pillow's prop to find

For these, oblivious of their own despair.

And soon its church with pallets rude was lined,

'Mongst which true priests of God all softly stole,

And sped with patriot prayers each parting soul.

CCLXXXII.

Just as the twilight swooned to lid-closed dark,
A stir was heard without; and striplings four,
Whose breasts had 'scaped the foeman's deadly mark,
Into the nave a goodly body bore,
Stretched on a litter, seeming stiff and stark,
Whose torn red shirt was steeped in redder gore,
And to whose beard and hair of iron grey
The death-dews clung, like silvery mist to spray.

CCLXXXIII.

Behind them, close walked Miriam, on whose brow
Black thunder-sorrow brooded, but whence dropped
No tear of feeble anguish even now.
And at the sight each prostrate sufferer propped
His head upon his hand, and breathed a vow
Of dying love towards her. But she stopped,
Nor looked on either side, and followed pale
The mournful convoy to the altar rail.

CCLXXXIV.

There with arresting hand she bade them pause,

And on the altar steps to lay him down,

And to a servant of dear Christ's sweet laws

Who wore the saintly Francis' habit brown,

Signalled ; and as distressful beauty draws

Even the heart that wears the chaste cold crown,

He hastened towards her and said lovingly,

"My daughter dear, what can I do for thee ?"

CCLXXXV.

"Wed me," she said, "dear father, to this man ;

Wed me this hour, ere he be man no more !

See ! though his eyes be closed, his cheeks be wan,

And though he soon will tread the heavenly floor,

He lives—he breathes ! his sinking bosom can

Receive the vows I long therein to pour,

Ere he doth leave me but a deaf-eared clod,

And goes to claim me at the Throne of God !"

CCLXXXVI.

The monk bent over the mute, hueless face,

And laid his ear against the blood-stained breast;

Then turned to her, and said: "Fair child of grace,

'Tis true that life hath not yet left its nest,

But even now for its true dwelling-place

Its wings it lifts, to fly away to rest.

'Twould be as though thou wedd'st a corpse, to wear

Eternal widowhood on thy young hair."

CCLXXXVII.

"O yes, I know!" she quickly did repeat,

In words that burst once more through sorrow's dam,

"Father, I know! But wed us, I entreat,

That I may plead, through him, before the Lamb,

For our wronged land! It, corpse-like at my feet,

I ne'er can be more widowed than I am!

I—I—will live to plot, he die to pray,

That Heaven and Earth conjoined avenge this day!"

CCLXXXVIII.

The trembling friar took up the clammy hand,
Whose pulse beat faint, and laid it within hers,
Whilst she repeated, at his grave command,
The solemn pledge which deathless bond avers.
And, on the instant,—o'er a silent land
As a faint breeze sometimes in summer stirs,
Then drops,—so Gilbert, for a moment's space,
Opened blue eyes, and smiled into her face.

CCLXXXIX.

Then grief had all its way, and wild she flung
Her body on his body, and loud wept;—
Wept with the loosened nerves, late overstrung,
And with the passion that too long had slept;
Whilst sympathetic horror stole among
The close-packed pallets. Some from out them crept,
Near her to kneel; and those who could not stir,
Died, weeping tears and blood for Rome and her

CCXC.

Stupendous Power! That, secret and afar,

Sitt'st on Thy throne, where none may come to Thee,

Oh! fling the gates of hidden heaven ajar,

That, for one moment, suffering flesh may see

Thy face, and what Thy darkened judgments are!

Are war, and sin and sorrow, Thy decree?

Is Fate our Father?   Thou art supremely strong,

And we, so weak!   How long, O Lord! how long?

CCXCI.

Now far and wide the sterile-rolling plain

Lay in the shadow of the passing Night,

Whose ebon wings, outstretched o'er land and main,

Move on,—slow,—silent,—none may mark their flight !

O'er stiff cold limbs for ever dead to pain,

O'er writhing forms whose cries still scared the kite

Calling for aid from those that, happier, slept,

On—on—unhalting, pitiless, she swept.

CCXCII.

There is a tall but crumbling tower that stands
Amid the lone Campagna's gloomiest waste,
Whose depths were dug by those Cyclopean hands
Which famed Cortona's massive circuit traced.
Above, its walls, like wrecks on littered strands,
Heaped more than built, rise up. Each age has traced
Its record on the masonry. Wouldst compare
Republic, Empire, ruin ?—Scan them there !

CCXCIII.

Its corner-stones are waifs from drownèd fanes,
Its mortar, marble gods. Urn, statue, bust,
All that of porphyry temples yet remains,
Tumbled and trampled, shattered, ground to dust,
Chipped, splintered, fouled, besmeared with wintry stains,
Into its chinks and crannies have been thrust.
Religions, dynasties, to patch a rent
In its rude mail, their sepulchres have lent.

CCXCIV.

The feudal bandit, 'scaping from the proof

Of bloody deed,—a later, fiercer Goth,—

Oft to its shelter fled with glowing hoof,

There fortress found, and braved a Pontiff's wrath.

Foxes and wolves have littered 'neath its roof.

But now alone, to sup his darnel broth,

And warm his agued limbs within its walls,

Thither at times the stricken shepherd crawls.

CCXCV.

To-night there was a little light within,

And, in the one sole chamber Time had spared,

Upon a pallet rough and mattress thin,

There lay a wounded man. His chest was bared,

But o'er his still clad form was thrown a skin

Such as Rome's minstrels wear,—rude, shaggy-haired,—

That served for coverlet ; and 'neath his head,

A sheaf of straw for pillow had been spread.

CCXCVI.

Soundly he slept, though ever and anon,

As though he would awake, he groaned and gasped;

But still a stout sword-hilt, from which was gone

One-half its blade, his right hand tightly grasped.

A little way aloof, her knees upon,

With folded palms in deep devotion clasped

Before a crucifix, herself had laid

Against the wall, a pale-faced Sister prayed.

CCXCVII.

And save these two, for many a league around,

No living mortal was: only the dead.

He, pierced and gashed, and plunged in sleep profound,

She, with her pure white veil around her head,

Between her God divided and each sound

That reached her ear from the poor sufferer's bed:

Her vigil's sole companion, one small lamp,

Such as you find in sepulchres old and damp.

CCXCVIII.

Sudden he woke, and with a battle-cry
Raising his body upright in the bed,
He brandished swift the shivered blade on high,
Struck at the foe, and rallied friends that fled.
He saw as yet with but half-waking eye,
And, bridging the abyss between the dread
Dark hour he fell and life's returning light,
Fancied himself still lost in thick of fight.

CCXCIX.

But when the air resisted not, nor stroke
Of quick-retorting sword attested fray,
Slowly to full-dawned consciousness he woke,
Stared weirdly round, and wondered where he lay.
He saw the bare blank walls, the nun's dark cloak,
The little oil-fed lamp's ascetic ray;
Then on his bootless hilt and bloody vest
Looking,—half he recalled, and read the rest.

CCC.

The pale-faced Sister, startled by his cries
'Mid her mute prayers, had risen from her knees,
And, with celestial pity in her eyes,
Stole towards the pallet, soft as steals a breeze
Through open casements just as sunset dies.
"Brother," she said, "I come to bring you ease,
To nurse your wounds and prop your tottering soul.
The fight forget: 'tis Heaven is now your goal."

CCCI.

Her eyes were cast down meekly, and she seemed
As one who saw yet saw not. On her brow
And round her lips a holy calmness beamed.
Yet surely, surely, not again, not now,
Not now,—as but a moment gone,—he dreamed
An empty dream? That face, that voice, avow
Herself, her soul! "Olympia!" loud he cried;
But on his lips all other language died.

CCCII.

She started, and flung up her arms, like one
Asudden through the brain in battle shot,
Or by some fearful tidings all undone.
"O Godfrid! Godfrid! Tell me it is not,
Not thou, not Godfrid! whom at rise of sun,
At noon, at night, I never have forgot
In my poor prayers! not thou, the once adored,
I see with shattered, sacrilegious sword!

CCCIII.

"Ah! yes, 'tis thou, sole vision of my heart,
Ere dearer Christ did fold me to His breast!
I must behold thee, even as thou art,—
His foe, His executioner confessed,
Stained with His blood. Oh! when we twain did part
On that smooth shore by smoother sea caressed,
How could I dream that we should meet as now,
A worse than brand of Cain upon thy brow!

CCCIV.

" Did all avail thee nothing ? Not the morn

When first we met, and thou with gracious speech

Didst sever from the stream-washed blossoming thorn

The snow-white branch, I, feeble, could not reach ?

Oh ! didst thou ne'er recall, in hours forlorn,

The loving ripple babbling on the beach,

Nor that all-trustful tenderness, which made

Thine alien presence welcome as I prayed ?

CCCV.

" Didst thou forget my little chapel quite ?

And did Madonna's statue, which thy hand

Helped me to deck, as swiftly fade from sight

As morning's footsteps from the evening's sand ?

Didst never, never, think thee of that night

Of raging tempest on a scourgèd strand,

When thou didst seek my face, and I did weep

To hear thy woe, and, blessing, bade thee sleep ?

L

CCCVI.

"Hide, hide that sword from sight! It pierces through
This heart of mine, I deemed could bleed no more.
Oh! how couldst thou that very hand imbrue
In Peter's blood, which, on the shining shore
'Twixt the grey mountains and the waters blue,
I linked with mine,—so, never linked before,
Or since,—when we together vowed our feet
Unto that pilgrimage, though vain, how sweet!

CCCVII.

"How often! oh how often! in the hush
Of solitary night, when spite of prayer
And kind Madonna's help the tears would gush
From my weak breast, I stifled my despair,
And from my cheeks the rolling drops would brush,
Hugging the hope that from thy memory ne'er
That pilgrimage would pass, but every scene
Would in thy heart remain for ever green!

CCCVIII.

"Thou hast forgot all,—all! Our journey dear,

Our simple mid-day meal, our evening halt,

The tumbling cataracts, the sheep-bells clear,

The tall black pine-woods scaling Heaven's vault,—

Tell me how soon did these all disappear,

How soon didst sow thy memory with salt?

When, when did cold oblivion begin?

And when was all as though it ne'er had been?

CCCIX.

"Well might my prayers, sin-weighted as they be,

Not reach the Throne of Grace. But thou, O thou!

Thou mightst at least have not been deaf to me,

And, for my sake, have reverenced the brow,

Mangled with thorns, of Him who died for thee!

Though thou believ'st not, was it hard to bow

To the remembrance of the words I spoke,

The tears I shed, the hoping heart you broke?

CCCX.

"No! all was vain. Shore, mountain, sea, and stream,
Milan's cathedral, Spiaggiascura's shrine,
The silent grief that worse than speech did seem,
To me so sacred, since it half was thine,
Then when we parted,—these were but a dream!
Alas! *I* dream not. Waking woe is mine,
Waking reproach. Forgive, O loving Lord!
That I once kissed the hand that grasps that sword!"

CCCXI.

Thus whilst she spake, he neither word nor sign
Let 'scape, nor muscle moved, nor eyelid dropped,
But, with lips parted, orbs all moist with brine,
Intently gazed and listened, till she stopped.
Then, one hand still, to hilt he held divine,
Clinging, his head upon the other propped,
Grave, he began: "With reverence hast not thou
Been heard, Olympia? Reverent, hear me now!

CCCXII.

"Deep in my heart thy sainted image lies,

And unforgotten, unforsworn has dwelt,

Undimmed, unchanged through change of time and skies,

The one sole memory just as keenly felt

Now, as when first thy presence stirred my sighs!

Nay, start not! shrink not! Though my soul should melt

In burning lava o'er thee,—not again,

Deem, I would fire the breast fired vainly then.

CCCXIII.

"Thou art the bride of Heaven, and I, alas!

Earthy; but, even as thou art heavenly, hear!

Oh! since that bitter parting came to pass,

Never an hour has been, in year on year,

Whether the hills were hoar, or green the grass,

Or dimpling corn uplifted playful spear,

Or mellow bunches drooped from branch and wall,

I had not sped to thee, hadst thou deigned to call.

CCCXIV.

"Forgot that morn! forgot that dewy spot,
Where Heaven, it seemed, dawned full upon my gaze
Forgot the little chapel! and forgot
Madonna's statue, at whose flowery base
With thee I knelt, my doubts remembered not!
Oh! if Oblivion from my brain shall raze
Record of these, then back may Mercy roll
Her opening gates, and shut them on my soul!

CCCXV.

"Nay! bear with me, Olympia, to the end!
Full well I know 'tis not thy love, thy wrongs,
With which thou dost reproach me, or that rend
The heart which henceforth but to God belongs.
Vainly I now should call thee more than friend;
Vainly, though every dear old feeling throngs
Back to my breast at sight of thee once more:
Vainly,—though e'en I knelt and could adore!

CCCXVI.

"Too late! Too late! Denied to me awhile,
For ever art thou ravished from me now!
Gone from thy lips the sweetly mortal smile,
And Heaven's pure snows defend thy sacred brow.
Thou art removed so far, thou wouldst beguile
My wildest vows, as did that virgin bough
Thy straining hands, when in the mountain glade
I lent my help! . . Alas! Me none will aid!

CCCXVII.

"Yet though thou didst abjure me, and hast given
Heaven all the love I once with Heaven did share,
The links which knitted me to thee, were riven
Tighter by time, and have survived despair.
I may from many sins need to be shriven;
But one weight still I shall not have to bear
Before the judgment-seat. My love was pure,
Even as thine, and did till death endure! '

CCCXVIII.

"I do upbraid thee not. Mayhap thou hast
Reserved a quiet cloister in thy soul
For memory of me and of the past,
Where Love's regretful dirges sometimes toll.
But when I learned thou hadst for ever cast
Hope to the winds, as men a torn-up scroll,
I looked around to find, or near or wide,
Some worthy work to do before I died.

CCCXIX.

"When thou didst seek a haven in the sky,
I, from my haven driven, put forth to sea.
And lo! from every tower and tocsin high,
Rang out the glad peal, summoning to be free,
Free or for ever slave, the land that I
Loved not the less, because it fathered *thee!*
Land, crowned with snow and girdled by the foam,
Fair as her Florence, outraged as her Rome!

CCCXX.

" Never, Olympia! since first couchant steel

Leaped from its sheath like lion from its lair,

Did pity plead, arm smite, or bosom feel

For Cause more sacred or divinely fair,

Than torn and mangled Italy's appeal.

Earth heard, but Heaven it was that crowned her prayer.

The stars our champions were, and with their smiles

Rescuing our swords, confounded tyrants' wiles.

CCCXXI.

"Bear with me, dear Olympia, bear alway,

If only for the sake of olden days!

Rome, still forgotten, still in fetters, lay.

I against thee as soon my sword would raise

As 'gainst the altar where thou kneel'st to pray;

And though I lift no voice of prayer or praise,

In half-believing awe my head I bow,

Before the Faith, that fosters such as thou!

CCCXXII.

"'Twas not against the altar I would fling
My feeble body, counting life as dross:
No, but from Peter's hampered hand to wring
The carnal sword, and leave therein the Cross!
That Rome, unswathed, may from the sepulchre spring,
And Italy no more bewail the loss
Of her first-born, but grouped around her knee
Her dear ones hail,—not fair alone, but free!

CCCXXIII.

"Ah! half in darkness on this earth we dwell,
Not in the light, but shadow, of the truth;
Confounding good with evil, Heaven with Hell,
Misjudging rage and hate for love and ruth.
But, though our souls thus vainly gnaw their shell,
And manhood seem but disillusioned youth,
I do believe, the lingering dawn despite,
That still we move, through liberty, to light!

CCCXXIV.

"Oh! if there be, for close of all this ache,

This panting struggle, a celestial goal,

Come with me there, Olympia! I will take

My blood-stained sword, and thou thy snow-white soul!

Perchance we there shall see that each doth make

Complete the other, and a godlike whole,

Hid by our human discords, flash to life,

In that pure atmosphere where dieth strife!

CCCXXV.

"But if I needs must go, leaving thee here,

Pass solitary, silent, to my doom,

I will await thee in whatever sphere

I may awake, of sunshine or of gloom.

For I will never, never yield thee, dear!

While soul surviveth! Meanwhile, tend my tomb;

And aye remember, that my latest breath

Blent, with thy name, the cry of 'Rome or Death!'"

CCCXXVI.

Faint came the final words, though tightly still

He grasped the widowed hilt she would release,

To join his hands in prayer. "Oh! do His will,

And with the Heavenly Victor make thy peace!

My heart shall keep a nook for thee, until

We meet i' the Land where wrong and sorrow cease.

But oh! bequeath me, ere thou leav'st me lone,

Some hope that we *may* meet before the Throne!

CCCXXVII.

"Thy words have meaning which thou dost not see.

All, all 'twixt Rome must choose, God's Voice hath said,

And endless Death!" "Then, Death," he cried, "for me!"

And waved his broken brand above his head;

Then dropped the hilt, and fell back heavily.

Dragged down by tears, she knelt beside the bed,

And 'gainst the offending hand laid sobbing cheek :—

For love too strong, for martyrdom too weak!

CCCXXVIII.

Now, with light jocund step, came young-eyed Morn,

Dancing and singing. o'er the eastern hill.

The timorous twilight, trembling, fled forlorn,

And in each thicket grove woke pipe and trill.

The world,—the old, worn world,—seemed freshly born,

Eden renewed, where man might drink his fill

Of brimming joy and beauty, nor e'er know

His naked self, that long bequest of woe!

CCCXXIX.

The sluggish mountains, donning crowns of gold,

Uprose to greet the morning. O'er the plain

Of blight and wreck a roseate wave was rolled.

Glowed in the sunlight aqueduct and fane,

No longer ruined. Happy Gods of old

Would soon, it seemed, their ancient seats regain,

And rule once more, from oracle and shrine,

A scene for mortal empire too divine!

CCCXXX.

Rome, Rome itself, bathed in auroral sheen,

Its domes, towers, columns, fanned by dewy gales,

Scanned from afar, one well indeed might ween

A sea of sunlight flecked with joyous sails.

Here, playful fountains leaped, and laughed between;

There, bright-trunked stone-pines spread their sombre veils

'Twixt earth and sky; the cracks in temples hoar,

But dimples seemed, with which they smiled once more.

CCCXXXI.

In narrow humid street, and open square,

Sun-flooded, gathered an unwonted throng;

And most where saint-crowned pillar clave the air,

Or spouting column soared like voice of song.

In every eye there lurked the angry glare,

In every nerve the self-suppression strong,

Of panthers ere they leap;—a fearful pause,

Ere bounds the body, and out-curve the claws!

CCCXXXII.

When, all at once, from lip to lip there flew
The rumour that the great Deliverer's tread
Nearer and nearer to the city drew,
Striding across the prostrate tyrant's head.
Some, shimmering in the distant sunlight blue,
Had seen his bayonet-tips and banners red,
Stream o'er the crests of the Nomentan Way;
And some, 'twas said, had heard his trumpets bray.

CCCXXXIII.

Then all the people started up, and took,
Hotly, their way unto the Eastern gate.
The comfortable cripple left his nook,
And hobbled with the crowd. With haughty gait,
Tall flower-girls dark their fragrant stalls forsook;
While timid maidens, fearing to be late,
Awaited not their mothers, but entwined
Their hands with baby boys, and ran like wind!

CCCXXXIV.

Yes! in the sunlight, pinnacles of steel
Flashed, and proud pennons fluttered in the air;
And from the ranks they crested, rang the peal
Of thunderous drum, and many a clarion's blare.
But, pitying Christ! what do those notes reveal,
And what these ensigns, waved anear, declare?
The Tyrant's pæan sounds 'neath banners black,
His hellish legions tramping in their track!

CCCXXXV.

On,—on,—they came, with rhythmic-moving tread,
His hirelings first, his Gallic prop behind;
And, last, with sullen step and unraised head,
A haggard, footsore file, whom Death unkind
Forgot to reap; who neither fell nor fled,
But, caught in toils no valour could unwind,
And reft of arms, now with the craven thong
Linking their limbs, toiled painfully along.

CCCXXXVI.

Just ere the vanguard of the proud array

The gateway reached, and bright warm bayonet-tips,

Dipping beneath its vault, from sheen of day

Passed, for a moment, into cold eclipse,

The crowd one last look gave, then slunk away :

The men with awful curses on their lips,

Women with silent anguish in their eyes,

And hate, in hearts of both, that never dies !

CCCXXXVII.

Then to the clang of cymbals, and the sound

Of triumph-breathing instruments, swept on

The exultant host through solitude profound :

Past silent-nodding wrecks of Empire gone,

Sallust's choked gardens, Cæsar's toppled mound.

What though bright fountains flashed, bright sunlight shone,

Loud pealed their trumpets, proudly waved their plumes,

Rome's dwellings seemed as empty as her tombs !

CCCXXXVIII.

But as they, onwards moving, roused the styes

Where Papal squalor supersedes the reign

Of Pagan ruin, swarms of black-robed spies,

Shavelings and sbirri, and their servile train,

Began through chink and crack with stealthy eyes

To peer and glance, as when from hole and drain

Foul-feeding vermin thrust suspicious snout,

Ere to their garbage-feast they sally out.

CCCXXXIX.

But when they saw the Cross-Keys waving high,

And heard Gaul's pompous music fill the air,

Then out they came in shoals,—a various fry:

Some in brown serge, with feet and foreheads bare,

And hempen cord whence hung the rosary;

Some robed in white, long-bearded, comely, spare,

Whose lofty brows roofed Learning and the Law;

And some, black-frocked, with clenched ascetic jaw.

CCCXL.

Sudden, as though from underground they sprung,

File after file, came troops of tonsured boys,

To whose slim bodies gaudy cassocks clung,

And who from native Freedom's healthy joys

Had, babes, been weaned, and taught an alien tongue.

Their pretty voices swelled the monkish noise;

Their tender forms, the sabre-sounding throng,

Their innocent hearts, the festival of wrong!

CCCXLI.

They too, the coiners of the spurious smile,

That round each victor's chariot skip and bark,

Obsequious hounds, the vilest of the vile,

Came thick; and those, who know not light from dark,

Meek, timorous hearts, whom fear and faith beguile,

And who in storm cling fast to Peter's ark:

And, last, the sceptic souls, who from them thrust

Man's genial dreams, and in the fasces trust.

CCCXLII.

So the armed host, by sycophant and slave,

Friar, and mendicant, and boyish band,

Followed and cheered, marched on with banners brave

To that famed spot on hoary Tiber's strand,

Where,—breathing emblem !—Christian statues wave

Over the stream forgotten Pagans spanned,

And Papal gaolers, copying the gloom

Of death, have carved a dungeon from a tomb.

CCCXLIII.

Across the bridge they streamed, an eager crowd,

And up the narrow squalid Borgo passed,

Till lo! the pile, whose head with sun and cloud

Converses, and whose feet are planted fast

In earth's foundations, rose before them proud,

Stupendous, soaring, dominant, and vast :

Type of that mighty Power which claims to quell

Man's soul, and rule the realms of Heaven and Hell.

CCCXLIV.

Then, as a stream that findeth wider bed,
Over the broad piazza loose they poured,
Between the curving colonnades, and sped
Up the long marble steps, defaced and scored,
Though polished smooth by many a pilgrim's tread ;
Until no more the glittering cupola soared
Up in the sky, and into shade they passed,
Like unto that the giant mountains cast.

CCCXLV.

A moment more, and 'neath the porch there pealed
Fresh music, and an army new drew near :
The Church's spiritual ranks, that wield
'Gainst Satan's host the crosier as a spear,
And on their bosoms wear the cross for shield :
Music that ravished the submissive ear,
And gorgeous companies, whose pompous train
Dazzled the eye, and dizzy left the brain.

CCCXLVI.

Troops of fantastic friars, endless files
Of eremites and missionaries brought
From sun-scorched lands and ice-engirdled isles;
Gold-mitred Abbots deep in prayer and thought,
And throne-defying Prelates wreathed in smiles,
Appareled in rich copes with gems inwrought;
And crimson-cassocked Cardinals, who curled
Aloft their heads, as though they swayed the world.

CCCXLVII.

Sudden shrilled silver trumpets, and there flashed,
At times as sunlight flashes, mailèd men,
Across whose doublets,—black with yellow slashed,—
Glowed plates of burnished steel, that dazed the ken.
Then brazen instruments and cymbals clashed,
Rending the lofty portico, and then,
So dread a sight approached, that they who saw
Dropped on their knees, and veiled their eyes in awe.

CCCXLVIII.

For in mid-air, by men upborne, there came,
Enthroned, a venerable man, arrayed
In more than regal glory. Eyes of flame,
Ravished from Juno's bird, his pathway made,
And, cushioned, shone his Triple Crown of fame.
Closed were his lids, but on his features played'
A more than mortal radiance ; and benign,
O'er the awed crowd he made the Holy Sign.

CCCXLIX.   ˙

When swept the long procession's final train
Into the august Temple's pillared nave,
Where statued pomp half baffles Death's disdain,
And wrings its boastful triumphs from the grave,
Army and concourse poured into the fane,
Distinguished now no more, but, like a wave,
Over the marble pavement rippling spread,
Till every slab was hid by human tread.

CCCL.

Then, with one voice, unto the Lord of Hosts,

Prince, priest, and people, deep Te Deum sang :

Who hurls the waves against the iron coasts,

Swells with His voice the dreaded tempest's clang,

And brings to nought the Mighty's impious boasts.

Loud through the spacious dome their anthem rang,

Whilst in the air without, with rhythmic stroke,

The accompanying cannon's bounding pulses spoke !

CCCLI.

But with these proud Hosannas, and the boom

Of insolent artillery that cleaved

Rome's arching sky, ascended too the gloom

Of orphaned hearths, beds widowed, lives bereaved ;

Where He eternally abideth, Whom

Eye hath not seen, ear heard, or heart conceived.

With awful eyes that scanned the nations wide,

Brooding He sate, His thunders by His side !

www.ingramcontent.com/pod-product-compliance
Lightning Source LLC
Chambersburg PA
CBHW030547040726
47497CB00008B/2614